a BLUE HARE in GUNDER'S GLADE

A BLUE HARE in GUNDER'S GLADE

TODD R. GUNDERSON

ILLUSTRATED BY ELLEN HOKANSON

wee b.
BOOKS

an imprint of W. Brand Publishing

NASHVILLE, TENNESSEE

wee b. books, an imprint of W. Brand Publishing.

j.brand@wbrandpub.com

www.wbrandpub.com

Printed and bound in the United States of America.

Cover design by designchik.net

Illustrations by Ellen Hokanson

A Blue Hare in Gunder's Glade / Todd R. Gunderson–1st edition

Available in Hardcover, Paperback, eBook, and Kindle

Hardcover ISBN: 978-1-950385-76-8

Paperback ISBN: 978-1-950385-72-0

eBook ISBN: 978-1-950385-73-7

Library of Congress Number: 2021944500

CONTENTS

Dedicated to my late uncle Richard C. Clark

and my aunt Esther

for their giving spirit through the years.

FOR THE READER

The early pioneers settling the prairies of the Dakota Territory came from many corners of the world; especially so, were those from the Scandinavian countries and Russian-Germans. Several of the characters in this story speak with harsh accents and improper English. I encourage each reader to imagine the voice of these characters and listen for the differences in dialect. Below are a few words and phrases used by characters in this story. Included here, are a few words from the Ojibwa/Chippewa language. There are other oddly spelled words, but you will find context for them within the reading.

Note: Norwegian and German have no "w" sound, so a "v" replaces many of these words where the characters would struggle.

NORWEGIAN	ENGLISH MEANING
Vi vil	Well
Juletre	Christmas Tree
Vigdis	Gunder's little sister

NORWEGIAN/ ENGLISH DIALECT	ENGLISH MEANING
Vill	Will
Vun	One
Dem	them
Dat	That
Motter	Mother

Vhen	When
Da	The
Dees	These

GERMAN	ENGLISH MEANING
Tannenbaum	Fir Tree or Christmas tree
Es geht dich nichts an.	It's none of your business.
Guten Abend	Good evening.
Es tut mir leid	I am sorry.

GERMAN/ENGLISH DIALECT	ENGLISH MEANING
Nozing	Nothing
Zis	This
Zere	There
Zee	The
Zome	Some
Und	And
Zoze	Those
Nozey	Nosey

OJIBWA/CHIPPEWA	ENGLISH MEANING
Boozhoo niij	Hello my, friend, Greetings
Waabooz	Rabbit, or snowshoe hare
Nanabozho	Cultural hero, spirit, or trickster in rabbit form.
Aaniin	Hello, or I see your light.

CHAPTER ONE

GUNDER'S REVELATION

Realizing how time had gotten away from him, Mike began sprinting across the open field toward the little town of Willow City, North Dakota. Bounding through a stubble sunflower field on the outskirts of town, he had wandered farther than he realized. With a desire for a little alone time, he had decided to trek north along the railroad tracks. The middle school boy found what he had been looking for, a jackrabbit, and it was hiding among thousands of large golden straws sticking out of the snow. Mike's new-found love was chasing jackrabbits, and he carried the usual Red Rider BB gun. But the 1942 model only scared the rabbits; the spring action was not strong enough to do any harm. It was his father's BB gun, and it was the only thing he had by which to remember him. Usually, he stayed close to his brother-cousin, as Gus called him, and didn't venture far. But this particular day was bright and white with a fresh coat of fallen snow blanketing the fields and the North Dakota plains.

Willow City was a small town, and it was not a long walk to be out of town in any direction. The railroad tracks he followed were a bit raised from the level fields, which gave him an advantage. The sight of a brown jackrabbit enticed him. Its ears, wiggling just above the snow, gave it away as it tried to stay out of sight among the cut sunflower stubble. He couldn't take the temptation any longer, and he leaped down the tracks and out after his prey. Of course, it was futile, as the rabbit was just too fast. After five or six attempts, following its tracks, and trying to get close, Mike noticed the time by the sun's appearance in the sky. It was nearly noon, and he was to unload a truck full of tires at his uncle's gas station before closing. Gus's father, Clair, took him in after a family crisis, so he was thankful and willing to help at the station. Rabbit chasing would have to wait.

He headed south, but it was a hard trudging run southward through the snow, and his short legs slowed to a slight trot as he approached a gravel road running east and west. Willow City was not far, but Mike was surprised to see an old man walking westward with a handful of groceries. The air was warm for a winter day, and the snow began to glisten from a slow melting across the surface. Mike knew that the evening's chill would harden it like ice by the next morning. Catching his breath for a few minutes, he waited for the man to get closer. Eventually, he recognized him as his Uncle Clair's friend.

"Hey there, Mr. Nilsen," Mike said as the man came within earshot of him.

"Is dat Mike?" he asked as he approached.

"Yep, it's me, Gunder," Mike said with pride.

"Young boy, vhat are you doin' out here by youself?" he asked in his Norwegian accent. "I haven't seen you for some time."

"I guess I got a little carried away chasing those jackrabbits," Mike confessed as he slung his BB gun around his shoulder using the old leather strap.

Suddenly, the old man's attitude turned bitter. "Oh, I hope you get every one, every one I tell you. You catch dem all and string dem up, chase dem avay, you vill," the old man said with a certain disdain. He sounded so angry, but Mike understood he was pointing his scorn at the rabbits.

Mike was surprised at the words. He had never heard someone talk about getting rid of all the rabbits. He knew that farmers didn't like them eating the alfalfa fields in some years, but this year was not bad for jackrabbits, and the farmers knew they needed rabbits to keep the coyotes fed. It was easier to deal with rabbits than to keep the coyotes off the herd. Even so, large rabbit populations would help the coyote's numbers grow, too, but only for a short while. Their populations bounced back and forth over the years. Mike realized that the rabbit population was down this year, but the birds of prey were numerous, and Mike had witnessed a hawk take a smaller rabbit earlier in the day. Farmers with chickens had a hard time with hawks, so rabbits were an important part of an ecosystem on the plains.

"You don't like rabbits?" Mike questioned.

"Vi vil, I sure don't tink da hares are good for me. Dey eat my juletre," the old man said. Mike had a hard time understanding Gunder, since he had not learned proper English as a boy. His father brought him to America when he was a teenager, and he had worked in the fields his whole life as a farmer.

"What's a u-la-trer?" Mike asked him as he cocked his head.

"Tannenbaum—da Christmas trees; my papa planted da trees."

"You look tired, Gunder; do you need help carrying your groceries? I can help you. You're still a long way from home," Mike said.

"Sure, I could use da help, young man."

"Don't you have a truck?" Mike asked him.

"It's not running, and I haven't da money to fix it," the old man said. "I tink somebody did someting to it, don't ya' know. I've bad luck arount my farm dees days," he confessed.

"What do you think is causing it?" Mike questioned.

Mike took the bags of groceries from him and began walking west toward his farm. His uncle would not mind him helping Gunder; he often encouraged Mike and Gus to help others around town.

The old man looked at him with thankful eyes and let out a sigh of relief as he shook his arms to lessen the cramping pain he was experiencing. "I vill tell you one ting," he said, then became quiet as they walked.

Mike waited for him to speak. He could see that he was thinking about what to say or how to say it. Suddenly, he began shaking his head and speaking strange phrases Mike had never heard before.

"Da hare bring bad luck vhen dey come. Blue he is, da color of da sky, a jinx on da hare."

"What did you say?" Mike asked. "I didn't catch that, Gunder. Are you talking about a jinx of some sort? Blue rabbits?"

"Oh, vi vil, I tell you like dis," he said. "Da blue hare has come to me at night, I know dis; I have seen vun. He brings bad luck to da farmer, you see. Da blue hare must go avay from here."

Mike had never heard such a story from anyone in the area. He could not understand why Gunder was saying these things to him. He had talked to him a few times but never heard this. Mike didn't want to ask any more about the hare stories. He did want, however, to understand what was going on, so he asked one last question, "Is there anything I can do to help you?"

"Vi vil, vonce the blue hare comes, he does not go avay vithout taking someting from you," Gunder said. "I fear he vill take my farm. You catch da blue hare, vill you, boy?" the old man asked.

"Where did you see a blue hare?" Mike felt forced to ask another question.

"I see vun dis fall, late, and I see two dis veek already. I see dem in my glade," Gunder stated. "You need my pop gun; I cannot see to use it vell. You get blue hare, ant I say dis, I give you pop gun."

"Okay, Gunder! I'll do my best to keep an eye out for 'em, but I've never seen a blue rabbit. As far as I know blue rabbits don't exist. This is 1959; I think every animal has been discovered. Plus, I'm sure everybody would love blue rabbits."

"NO!" Gunder said rather abruptly, startling Mike. "My sveet Vigdis vould not agree. She is no more since blue hare came to Trondelag! I give you pop gun if you get blue hare." He slowed as he spoke. "I knew vun day it vould return for me."

The look on Gunder's face showed anguish, and Mike didn't want to ask who Vigdis was. Whoever it was, they were no more, and he couldn't see bringing it up again. Furthermore, he didn't know the word Trongelag, so he drew the attention to the pop gun. Mike knew Gunder meant BB gun. He needed a new one, especially if it was better than the old Red Rider he had over his shoulder.

After some thought, Mike asked, "What kind of BB gun do you have, Gunder?"

"It is a Daisy, I tink, a 25," he said with question in his voice.

Mike's heart jumped inside his chest. He couldn't believe what he had just heard. A Daisy model 25 was a pump action BB gun, and he would do anything to get his hands on one.

Suddenly, a noise was heard behind them. It was an old Chevy truck headed west. It was Clair. They walked to the side of the road and waited. He pulled up beside them, opened the passenger door with a long stretch and joked, "This boy bothering you, Gunder?" he asked.

"Oh, no. He is kind enough to carry da bags for me," he replied.

"Jump in you two, and I'll take you home. I was going to pick you up earlier, but I had a customer to deal with," Clair said.

He drove Gunder to his farm about a half mile down the road. It was an easy place to find, for a large grove of pine trees flanked the small farm on all directions. Beautiful conical shaped trees, blue-green in color, stood tall as if guarding the small farmstead. So many of the same kind of tree seemed out of place on the North Dakota prairie.

Arriving in the drive, they let him out, and they carried his goods to the front door. Gunder thanked them both in his usual way and tried to give them money, but Clair refused. He had come for Mike anyway, as truth would have it.

"I'll come over soon and look for those blue rabbits, Gunder. Just give me a few days," Mike assured as he turned and waved.

Gunder's farmstead was small, but the buildings were very well maintained. A beautiful red barn stood off to the left of the house with the door facing east. The tools of the trade, tractors, plows, drills, and such, were set neatly in a row some distance behind the barn as not to be seen from the road. Mike noticed that many farmers in the area built their barns facing east. The morning sun illuminated the inside for those early risers and kept the grounds dry outside the door. It also provided even heating of the roof during the course of the day. The south side of the barn was protected from the harsh winds in the colder months and allowed sunshine to light the area all day. In the hot months, cattle could gather on the north side of the barn to remain cool and be separated from the

machinery. An old wooden grain storage building stood nearby. It was a funny-looking building
with the door high off the ground; stored grain
would not pour out when opening the door. The
house was painted white and was rather small. It
was built for only three people many years ago;
it was practical, winters were long and cold, and
the single fireplace could heat it well. An old outhouse on the right had nearly been overtaken by
spruce trees, but it remained in great shape. The
long stroll back to the truck had Mike wondering

ehakanson©

if Clair had come looking for him, but he got his answer rather quickly.

"Mike, you know I trust you, but you ventured a little far, don't you think? I'm surprised you were out as far as you were on foot. I was a bit worried about you. You left at 9:30 this morning. Aren't your feet cold?" Clair asked.

"Not at all, but I know I went too far. I'm sorry. I was chasing the jackrabbits . . . when I saw one," Mike replied.

"Jackrabbits? You mean the white tail? The brown ones? I haven't seen a lot of them around lately," Clair said.

"They're out there, maybe not a lot, but enough to get my attention." Mike laughed. "I want to ask you a question, Uncle Clair. Gunder told me a story about a blue hare, and I—"

Clair interrupted him sharply. "I heard what you said. Don't ask that old man any more about the blue hare! Just don't do it! You won't hear the end of it."

"Why, Clair, why?" Mike begged.

"Keep this between you and me, okay, Mike?" Clair asked as they got in the truck.

"Sure."

Clair put his attention to backing out of the drive and proceeded down the road. Mike knew he was also thinking about what to say, and he eventually spoke. "Mr. Nilsen and I have sat for many hours down at the station on the slow days. We've talked about a lot of things, but the saddest story has to be the one he tells about the blue rabbits of Trondelag, Norway."

"Trondelag? What is that?" Mike asked. "I think he tried to tell me about it when you were coming down the road."

"You're lucky I came when I did, then." Clair laughed. "I saved you from a long walk with an angry man."

"What's Trondelag?" Mike asked again.

"It's a county in Norway where Gunder was born. He was from a very rural area up in the hills of Norway . . . Trondelag. They raised a special kind of sheep there called the grey troender. I'm just telling you what he told me, Mike, that's all. Anyway, their sheep started to die around the same time a blue hare was seen in the area. Other members of the community had the same problem.

Apparently, his uncle killed a very large one and mounted it on the wall. Eventually, Gunder's little sister died of a strange illness, and just before she died . . . she turned blue. Gunder's father blamed it on the Cerulean Rabbits, or hares as he likes to say, and moved his family away to America. Gunder was a young teenager when he got here."

"What's cer–roo–le–an?" Mike asked.

"Oh, that's just another name for sky blue. You know, the azure blue color," Clair said.

"Did it really happen, Clair?"

"Mike, Gunder told me that for the last ten years. Sometimes he doesn't know when to stop talking about it. The story changes a little bit every time he tells it, well, maybe it doesn't change, but he adds to it; that's for sure. I can't help but believe every word. I can't explain a blue rabbit, but I know it did happen. He lost his younger sister to a strange disease. I knew his father when I was younger; he mentioned his daughter, Vigdis, many times—his wife did, too. I saw her cry in the old hardware store once, back when they sold furniture. Gunder's mother was staring at a wall painting hanging in there. It was painted with cerulean blue. I remember the picture well because my grandmother bought it. It was a copy of *A Girl with a Blue Watering Can*. Old Mrs. Nilsen said it was her daughter in the picture. She just couldn't get the blue out of her mind. I remember them having to help her to the truck."

"Where have I been? There's a lot to this story. I can't believe I've never heard it before," Mike said.

"Mike, you're young, and you weren't always here, you know. And really, Gunder's been pretty quiet about it lately. Ask Gus, I think he's heard it; just don't go telling everybody ya" know," Clair said.

"I'll ask him in the nest tonight; we have a meeting," Mike said.

"But that's not all, Mike. To make matters worse, Gunder's father had moved his family to England due to their great love for sheep ranches. He took a job in a rock quarry to raise money for the purchase of a new ranch. The job was in the Portland England rock quarries. And get this, Mike, everybody in Portland was afraid of rabbits. You can't even say 'rabbit' there. It's the truth. Your great aunt, Ingrid, was from England, and I asked her about it," Clair stated. "She knew all about it. The quarries had a few accidents, and they blamed the rabbits for burrowing holes in the ground and causing rockslides and such. So, Gunder grew up with this . . . fear of rabbits . . . or, at the least, just not liking them too much."

"How did they get *here*, Clair?" Mike asked.

"Well, Gunder's father learned about the government land grants in America. I guess he figured he could get a lot more land here, so he eventually moved his family to America. Gunder told me they had a lot of sheep for a while, but it was too cold in the winter. They focused on farming. Gunder took over the farm when his mother and father passed away," Clair explained.

"Uncle Clair, there have been years with lots of rabbits in the fields. I remember when I first came to live with you; there were jackrabbits everywhere," Mike said.

"I know, Mike. Those were the years I made a lot of money on huntin' shells. Gunder was no exception. He was in the store every week buying some. I remember one week when he bought a shirt with a padded shoulder from Mr. Anderson at the hardware store. And one year he bought a 10-gauge from the Montgomery Ward's catalog. He fired that thing every hour all night long. Some of the neighbors up there had a few words with him." Clair chuckled a bit.

"What's a 10-gauge?" Mike asked.

"Oh, just a very loud shotgun to scare the critters away from his Christmas trees. His father had started planting trees for an eventual tree farm which would add income in the winter, and it went well for a number of years—"

"Let me guess," Mike interrupted, "the blue rabbits came."

"Well, rabbits, in general, came. They destroyed all the young trees they had planted that fall. It was a cold winter with a lot of snow. They ate nearly an acre of spruce trees. His father got sick that winter, and Gunder didn't replant that section. It's a beautiful glade now, right in the middle of his forest of pines. But he sure gave it a whirl with that old 10-gauge. Some of the other farmers used them in their sunflower fields to keep the birds out. They're very annoying close to town, and they don't feel good on the shoulder," he said with a laugh. "You can talk to Gus, but don't ask old Gunder about the blue rabbits, okay?"

Mike nodded his head as they got out of the truck, having arrived back at the station. Mike started his work but pondered on the blue rabbits for much of the day.

CHAPTER TWO

Mike's Meeting

G us arrived as Mike rolled the last tire into the station. He had several large tires piled in the corner waiting for an extra hand.

"It's about time you got here. I can't lift these into the rack by myself," he said in a huff.

"It's not my job. You took this on yourself, remember?" Gus retorted.

"I know, I know, but will you please help me lift them up?" Mike pleaded.

"Okay, but you'll owe me."

With the tire unloading complete, Mike collected his wages from his Uncle Clair, and the boys left for the Iceberg Diner. It was time for some ice cream. "You can buy me some ice cream for helping you with the tires," Gus said as they walked past a few doors up the street.

"I guess that's fair," Mike replied.

As the boys reached the door of the diner, they arrived at the same time as a young Chippewa girl. The boys stepped back a few steps to clear the way of the entrance. She walked in ahead of them as Mike held the door for her. She was dressed nicely in cowboy boots, blue jeans, and a yellow blouse, and she was wearing an open-style western coat.

"*Miigwech.* I mean, thank you," she said as she looked at Mike in a sweet, shy way. She bowed her head to hide her face. She found her way to the

corner table, sat down, and raised her head enough to glance at Mike again. Gus caught her looking at Mike and noticed a smile across her face.

"Mike, did you catch that? She smiled at you!" Gus whispered as he punched Mike's arm.

"Cut it out, Gus. Leave me alone. No ice cream for you, then," Mike said with an embarrassed look.

"Hey, guys," a voice came from the back of the diner. It was Deevee and Levi Wagner; their mother owned the diner, and they were washing dishes like so many times before.

"I see you're doin' the dishes again. I'm glad my mom doesn't own a diner." Gus laughed.

"Can we get a couple of bowls of ice cream, Deevee?" Mike yelled to Deevee as they found a seat at the counter. Lowering his voice, Mike whispered, "That girl took our spot."

Deevee walked up to Mike and leaned in. "Do you know her? She came in earlier with a woman, but I've never seen her before."

"No, I've never seen her until today. She must be new around here. So, how about the ice cream; can I get some?" Mike asked changing the subject.

He had noticed the girl looking at him but wasn't interested in any conversation. Only one thought replayed in his head, and it rehearsed the telling of Gunder's story in the nest.

The nest was the boys' meeting place. It was an attic in an old filling station on Main Street. It had been vacant for a number of years, and the owner didn't seem to mind them being there. They figured he liked having somebody watching the place. The boys could enter through a window on the alley side and climb a wall studded ladder into the attic. It was warm in the winter close to the roof, and one end had plenty of natural light cascading in through the gable vents. The boys would walk a precarious route to the north end amid old oily rags, boxes, cans, and old car parts from years past. Gus usually sat in an old rocking chair while the boys surrounded him on old metal buckets. But Mike would take the rocking chair tonight, or he would not tell his story.

"Deevee, get Levi; I've got something to tell you," he said, taking his bowl of ice cream from him.

Deevee handed Gus a bowl, too. "What is it?"

"What is it?" Levi also asked as he arrived.

The four boys were all staring at each other, two on either side of the counter. "I'm calling a meeting in the nest tonight. You have to come. I have some news to tell you, and you're going to think I'm crazy," Mike said. "Only thing is, I'm sittin' in the rocking chair tonight."

"It better be good, Mike," Gus said with a sneer. "I hate those old buckets."

"Oh, it will be, and you should already know some of it," he said to Gus. Gus looked at Mike carefully but said nothing.

"Sir?" the young girl called from the corner table.

"Yes, can I help you?" Deevee said with a slight stutter. His mother went out for a short errand, and he was left in charge, mainly to do the dishes, but he could get the smaller items a customer might want.

"May I ask a question?" She spoke with a quiet tone; Deevee nodded. "Do you have some outdated vegetables you were throwing out? I could use them to feed some farm animals I have," she said.

"Oh, well . . . umm . . . I guess. I'll check with the owner when she comes back in. It will only be a minute. She ran across the street to buy some more scrubbing rags from the hardware store," Deevee said a bit shyly.

The door of the diner came open, and the bells on the door jamb rang announcing her return. Deevee and Levi's mother walked in holding a large package of towels and several other cleaning agents, but her coat sleeve caught the top of a chair which toppled her load. The young Chippewa girl rushed to her aide, as did the boys. Setting the items on the counter, Deevee asked his mother the girl's question about old vegetables.

"Well, I have a few old things that need to go, but I'm not sure any old animal will eat it," she said. "Come with me to the back room." She motioned for the girl.

The boys finished their ice cream, and the four settled on a time to meet in the nest. Five o'clock couldn't come fast enough for Mike, but the Wagner boys had to finish helping their mother. Mike and Gus waited for the boys at the Cenex station. They helped Clair fix a few cars with minor issues and pumped gas for other customers. Mike thought more about how he wanted to share the news. He wanted, so badly, to have something the boys could investigate. Finding a blue rabbit that was making Mr. Nilsen upset was worth trying to help. Plus, Mike could get a nice BB gun if things worked out well. He was sure Gunder was seeing a gray version of the brown jackrabbits out on the prairie or around the grain bins on his farm. Mike had seen several shades of fur on the jackrabbits before, and some of them were gray in color mixed with some brown. Gunder admitted his eyes were not that good, so maybe he was just seeing things. The hope was to catch a rabbit gray enough to pass for a shade of blue in order to trade Gunder for a BB gun. Mike didn't believe in blue rabbits, but the others could not know that just yet.

The five o'clock meeting in the nest was nearing, and Gus and Mike met the Wagner boys in front of the diner. They followed the sidewalk heading to the old filling station. The evening air was colder, the sun had lowered in the sky, and a few snowflakes glowed in the evening sun. A single bench decorated the edge of their town's tiny park, and on it sat the Chippewa girl they had met earlier in the diner. Mike began crossing the street. He didn't want to have a conversation with her in front of the other boys. He knew they would tease him if he showed interest. His determination to get to the nest intrigued the boys, and they followed after him in a slight trot. "Wait up!" Levi called. "Mike, what's the hurry?" Deevee asked loudly. Mike glanced back at the girl on the bench, and their eyes met. She quickly looked down again.

The boys tromped up the alley and jumped through the back window of the old filling station, climbed the slats nailed to the studded wall, and entered a hole in the ceiling. They made their way to the north side of the attic. It was cold and getting darker, so hidden flashlights were taken from a box and quickly turned on.

They spoke in a whisper to each other about the girl on the bench. They could see her from the attic through the louvers on the front gable vent. She shivered from the cold.

"Who's she waiting for?" Gus asked.

"That's strange; I've never seen her here before," Levi said. "She sure looks cold."

As they watched her from their upper perch, a black pickup truck appeared. It stopped in front of the bench, and a woman addressed her.

"Did you find him, Omi?" the woman asked from the truck with great concern. "I have seen nothing, sweetheart."

The boys gathered around the vent tightly and turned off their flashlights; they listened to the conversation from their upper perch.

"No, Mother. I have not seen him anywhere. I have given up and want to go home," she said. Her voice had a sad pitiful sound as she sat down on the seat of the truck. The boys watched the two travel a few blocks west and turn north.

"I bet they bought the Anderson place," Gus said. "Remember Gary Anderson, the senior who was so good in math? His family moved to Montana last year. Their house has been for sale for a long time. I'll bet that's where she's stayin'. She mentioned farm animals. It's on the edge of town, and there's a large barn in the back of the place."

Mike decided to get the meeting started and changed the subject quickly with an interesting phrase. "The Blue Rabbit Mystery," he said with *mystery* in his voice.

"What did you say?" Deevee asked with a strange look on his face.

"Sounds like you've been hangin' around old Gunder Nilsen," Gus said with a laugh.

"Yes, I have," Mike returned quickly.

"Oh, no! Are you kidding me, Mike? This is about the blue hare in Gunder's glade?"

"Gunder's glade?" Mike asked. "What's that?"

"That's the clearing in the pine trees behind his house. He's got this big old Christmas tree farm on his property with a beautiful meadow out in the middle," Gus said. "That's where he saw the first one a few years ago. They haven't cut trees from the farm for years."

"Wait, wait, wait, you guys. Somebody tell me what you're talkin' about. Will somebody explain?" Levi asked.

"Yeah, I'm lost, too," Deevee chimed.

"Okay, Gus, let me do the talkin'. Everybody sit down for a second. Today, I walked with old Gunder Nilsen. I helped him with his groceries, and he told me there are blue rabbits on his property.

His family moved here from Norway after his little sister turned blue and died. They blamed the rabbits, some kind of jinx or somethin'. He says they'll ruin his life with bad luck and stuff. He wants me to catch the blue rabbits; actually, he doesn't care what happens to 'em. But I get a new BB gun if we can catch one," Mike finished.

"There ain't no blue rabbits out there," Levi said.

"I don't think there is, either, but I did see some gray ones. I think that's what he's seein'," Mike said.

"All I know is Dad told me to stay away from him. Levi, did dad tell you that, too?" Deevee asked.

"I don't think so, 'cause I've never heard nothin' about the blue rabbits." Levi shrugged.

"Well, I have!" Gus said. "That old man scared me a few years ago when I was younger."

The other boys snickered at him, and Deevee tried to push him off his bucket. "Did you cry, Gussy Poo?" he asked. The other boys laughed.

"Not so fast, boys. I'll tell you what Gunder told me. Then you'll take that back."

The boys stopped laughing, and Gus steadied himself and stood up, pulled Mike out of his rocking chair, and sat down. He placed the flashlight between his legs pointing it upwards. Strange shadows formed across his face, and an ominous voice accompanied the start of the tale. "One night several years ago, Dad and I were working late. Gunder tapped on the glass of the service door and wanted in. The shop was closed, but Dad opened it. Gunder wanted 10-gauge shells, so Dad sold him some, but asked him not to shoot at night. From what I understand, he didn't listen."

"Was it for his shotgun?" Levi asked.

"Don't interrupt, Levi," Gus said. "Anyway, before Gunder left, he told us a tale I'll never forget. Gunder said his great uncle hunted rabbits, really big rabbits. The biggest rabbits in the world, only found in Norway. He bagged a big one and mounted it on the wall, but after several months, the thing started turnin' blue right there on the wall. They got used to seein' it like that and never really noticed how blue it was. It was after that, other blue rabbits started comin' around the little farmyard, scaring the sheep, eating their corn and crops, getting into the garden, and digging all kinds of holes everywhere. He said his uncle fell in one and was never seen again. The hole didn't have a bottom to it. The rabbits were blue, and they couldn't see 'em at night. Neighbors said he had bagged the alpha male and the others wanted revenge."

"Aww, come on, Gus," Deevee said with disbelief. "Giant blue rabbits; do you really believe that?"

"All I can say is, my dad's heard many of the stories, and he believes a lot of it. Gunder's too convincing. After what I heard, I didn't go around him anymore. It's scary the way he talks. Deevee, something happened, 'cause Gunder cried that night when he told us the jinx got his sister; she turned blue—and died!" Gus opened his eyes wider than usual, the bright light still shining in his face.

"I'd cry, too, if my sister died. That's normal, Gus. Why should that scare you?" Levi said in his logical way.

"That's right, Gunder told me the same thing about his sister when we were walking, so that part of the story hasn't changed," Mike said.

"Guys, if we have the blue rabbit mystery here, then Gunder brought it. Maybe we better watch out for our lives!" Gus said with meaning.

"You're still scared, Gus. I can't believe it. I just want a new BB gun—well, a better one, anyway," Mike said. "I ain't scared of no blue rabbit. I was chasing those things all morning. They run for dear life when they see ya'. I've never seen one run at me; if they did, I'd boot 'em in the cottontail."

The others laughed and joked, and Deevee stood up and practiced kicking his boot. "Should I kick 'em side-boot or straight on?" He laughed.

Mike took charge again and pulled Gus out of the rocking chair. He sat down and asked the group for a vote. "Are you with me on this, guys? Tell me you'll help me find a blue rabbit for old Gunder. Raise your hands."

The boys raised their hands, but Gus added, "I'm not touching a blue rabbit!"

CHAPTER THREE

A GIRL'S TROUBLE

The next morning was Sunday, and during the night, a fresh coat of white fluffy snow had fallen. Gus and Mike eventually met the other two boys on the back steps of the diner. Their parents always had breakfast at the diner on Sunday mornings, as did many other families. Mr. and Mrs. Wagner worked together to cook for the morning guests. Pancakes, sausage, eggs, and even bowls of Cream of Wheat were favorites at the diner. Dee-vee and Levi were expected to help with the dishes from time to time. Sunday Morning was one of those times; families attending church services were always in early. The boys were no exception. They never missed Sunday school class because if they did, Miss Edith would assign homework, and then share it with their parents who made sure they did it.

Gus and Mike caught a look at the Farmall Cub tractor Deevee and Levi had driven into town after their parents had left the house. While driving into town, the boys had taken turns riding on a long wooden toboggan attached to the rear hitch with a long hemp rope. Mike wanted a ride. He could still smell the warm scent of fuel coming from the engine as they sat on the cold steps in the back of the diner.

"I know why they call it the Iceberg Diner," Mike said with a shiver in his voice. "But I still want a ride on that toboggan."

Deevee ran into the diner and received permission to go for a short ride, but before Mike realized what was happening, Deevee ran out and the others jumped on the sled before Mike had a chance.

"Wait a minute; I'm the one who wanted to ride the sled. Why do I have to drive?" Mike protested, but it was too late. Somebody had to drive the first leg.

Mike had driven the tractor numerous times out on their ranch but driving in the snow was different. The large tires, rolling over the snow, kicked up the fluffy flakes into the faces of the boys on the toboggan. Mike took great pleasure turning them into white snowmen as he found just the right places with deeper snow through which to drag them. They laughed and yelled, "Faster!" but the tractor was going at top speed. He swayed and turned and occasionally tipped them off in a ditch or low spot, but they ran and jumped back on just as fast as they had fallen off. Mike stopped the tractor at the intersection near the church. The tractor sat still for a moment and Mike stared off into the distance. The boys assumed Mike wanted to ride on the sled, and they began fighting over who would be the next driver. It soon became apparent that Mike was a little preoccupied as he ignored his name.

"What are you lookin' at, Mike?" Gus asked as the others took notice. "Mike? Oh, Mike? Are you with us Mikey?" Gus said again.

Levi jumped up, shook the snow off his coat, and aimed his head in the same direction. "He's watching that new girl across the way, the one we saw yesterday."

"Not so loud, Levi!" Mike finally responded. "I'm just trying to see what's going on over there. It doesn't seem right. They're running all over the place. Just watch with me for a minute."

Forgetting about the cold, the boys all took notice. The girl was on her hands and knees looking under the black truck parked in the driveway. Then, she ran around the side of the barn and back again. Her mother searched various side buildings and around the house looking in doors and lifting objects in the yard.

"They're looking for something, I guess," Mike said. "I'm going over there to help."

"No, you're not, Mike!" Gus said. "We only have a few minutes before the church bells ring."

"I don't see a lot cars here yet," Mike said. "We still have twenty minutes I'll bet."

"Let him go. I'm wondering what they're doing too," Deevee said.

Mike jumped down off the tractor and ran across the snow-covered church lot and across the street.

"You better not be late for Sunday school!" Gus yelled.

The other boys were cold but decided to take one last ride. Deevee took the wheel and made one more run up and down the street then headed for the diner to clean up.

Several hours later, Mike eventually came into the diner, but most had left. His uncle, Clair, was sitting in the corner, sipping on a hot cup of coffee. "Mike, come over here right now!" he ordered in a rather disgruntled manner. "You know where you were supposed to be? Where have you been? You've missed Sunday school, and you missed Father Beckman's Christmas message. Miss Edith has already given me your homework. I'm very disappointed in you."

"Uncle Clair, you've always said to help others when there was a need. Well, I was helping that new girl who moved into the Anderson place. She was crying; I had to help!" Mike poured out his heart.

"What was wrong with her? And, before you start, you used that excuse with me yesterday when you were helping Gunder," Clair said. He leaned forward and placed his coffee cup down sternly waiting for Mike to speak.

Suddenly, the front door of the diner flew open, and the other three boys whisked in. "Mike, Miss Edith wanted to know why you weren't in Sunday school. Where were you? You lost a star!" one of the boys railed.

"Mike, what happened over at that girl's place?" Gus asked. The other boys pounded him with more questions.

"Well, what was it?" Gus pushed him. Clair stood up, looked at them all, shook his head in disdain, and walked away.

"Spit it out!" Levi said.

"Okay, stop! Keep it down and I'll tell ya'," Mike said. He gathered himself and sat down on a diner stool. "Ominotago is her name, but she goes by Omi for short. She was crying a lot when I got there. I asked her if I could help, but she wouldn't look at me. I guess she was embarrassed or somethin'."

"What was wrong over there?" Deevee asked quickly. Clair decided to come back to hear the story and stood with his arms folded in frustration behind Mike. He didn't seem amused.

Mike began again but seemed to measure his words before speaking them. "After her mom told me the problem, she finally started talkin'. Another one of her rabbits is missing. That's what she was lookin' for last night. Remember when she was on the bench by the park. We watched from the nest when her mother came by. She was lookin' for a rabbit then, too. She thinks somebody let this one out of its cage during the night."

"How many does she have?" Gus asked.

Mike took a deep breath. "She's got six left in the barn in the back stall. And there's no way for

'em to get out of that place. I saw it. They have straw and water, but they can't get out. They're pure white bunnies. Nice big bunnies. She loves those rabbits."

"Sounds like you got to know her a little, Mikey," Gus teased.

"You can tease me all you like; I like her. She's really sweet. She wants to be my friend. I helped her take 'em out of the cages and put them in the back stall."

"Whatever you do, don't tell her about the nest, Mike," Deevee cautioned. "No girls!"

"Don't worry, but I'm going over there after lunch, and I told her I was gonna bring you guys. So, I'll pick you up here when I go. I think Gus will come with me. Looks like you'll be doin' dishes with your mom right now," Mike said. The diner was nearly empty, but dishes remained on most of the tables as was usual for Sundays.

Clair unfolded his arms. "Mike, sounds like you know how to make friends. I wish that would rub off on Gus here," he said as he rubbed his head. "Let's get back to the house. Mother will have some things for us to do, too, but that comes first. You boys can leave after your chores and lunch. Oh, and don't think I'll forget about you playing hooky from Sunday school, Mike. You'll pay for it with your time."

"Yes, sir," Mike said. He hoped Clair would eventually forget about it, but he knew better. He had really disappointed him this time.

After morning chores and an eventual good home-cooked afternoon meal, Gus and Mike bundled up in their wool jackets and started out for the diner. They hoped Deevee and Levi were finished with the dishes. Mike was excited to see Omi again, and Gus could tell they wouldn't be waiting long if they weren't ready. Hoping to see them waiting in a booth, Gus pushed the diner's door open and tried to walk in, but Bern Ebner met them in the doorway.

"Goot afternoon, young boys," he said. Bern was a tall, middle-aged German man who lived near Gunder Nilsen northwest of Willow City. He was a hard-working farmer, as was his entire family. He had been in America for years, but with so many German relatives nearby there was no need to learn proper English. Like Gunder, he had a thick accent, but he looked like any other hard-working farmer around Willow City. His German-English was hard to follow at times.

"Good day, sir," the boys said in unison.

As he stood before them, the boys noticed his dirty hands. They were indeed dirty, but the boys knew he was a hard-working farmer, and oil and grease-soaked hands were hard to scrub clean at times. Still, they were noticeably stained.

"Looks like you've been working hard, Bern," Gus said making reference to his hands.

Bern looked at him strangely and noticed the other boy eying his hands as well. He lifted one and spoke. "Zat is nozing you should vorry about, boyz. Vee all do vhat vee gotta do." He said his good-byes, and the boys watched him as he stepped out and turned toward the Cenex station. He forced his hands in his pockets but looked back through the glass of the diner's front window at Mike.

"What did he mean by that?" Mike asked.

Gus shrugged. "Who knows? I guess I should've kept quiet."

Deevee and Levi were eating ice cream at the counter, but their mother grabbed two bowls for Gus and Mike, too, as she told them to sit. "Thank you!" they said as they plunged their spoons deep into the treats.

"I don't care how cold it is outside, ice cream never goes out of style," Mike said. "But we better hurry 'cause I told Omi we'd be along sooner than later."

"Why are we going over there, Mike?" Deevee asked.

"I can't help but think there's a rabbit thief in this town. We're gonna help her find her rabbits. Somebody's gonna pay for stealing," he replied with a mouth full of ice cream.

"You and rabbits. You were chasing rabbits yesterday, too. What are you, some kind of rabbit detective?" Levi asked. The other boys laughed, and Gus choked on his mouthful.

Mike was offended by the comment and placed his hands on his hips. "We have a chance to make a good friend—well, at least I do. It does have to do with rabbits, but I'm sure it's just a coincidence. Chasing rabbits yesterday has nothin' to do with Omi. Her rabbits are white, not jackrabbits. But something is very wrong. Omi shouldn't be missing two rabbits. She's too good to them to be careless, and it's not easy to open those cages. I think somebody took 'em."

"Who knew she had rabbits?" Levi asked.

"That's a good question," Mike said.

Deevee had to add his two cents. "You want us to help you look for blue rabbits on Gunder's farm, and now you want us to look for rabbits in town. Where did the rabbit thing come from all of a sudden? Don't you think that's a little strange, Mike?" He ended with a little giggle.

"We'll just walk around a little with Omi and make her feel better, that's all guys. You can do that, right?" Mike asked.

"The Hairy Farmer's Daughter gets hungry at night, Mike. Maybe she ate those rabbits," Levi said with a smirk.

"Levi!" his mother called from the end of the counter. "Be nice, and I don't want to hear any noise about The Hairy Farmer's . . . well, you know. That'll be enough of that. You boys get going now, and help Mike make a new friend," she said.

The boys scraped their bowls clean and walked out as if they had tails between their legs. "How much does she know about Omi?" Mike asked angrily.

"Oh, I told her at lunch today. I told her about you runnin' off this morning. Doesn't matter; she thinks it's cute, Mikey," Deevee said with a tease. The others laughed as they headed for the Anderson place.

The afternoon air seemed to be getting colder, and the boys buttoned their coats to their necks and turned their collars up as they walked west along Main Street and north towards Ominotago's house. There had been little foot traffic on the sidewalks west of the church, and walking in the snow became harder. The boys could see the old gray barn in the back of the Anderson house and a few outbuildings on the grounds. Each boy was scanning for rabbits as they walked, but Gus soon asked the obvious question.

"How are we gonna see white rabbits in all this snow?"

"Like I said, don't worry about it. I'm just going to introduce you to her and show you the other rabbits. I don't really want to remind her about the lost ones, so don't say anything." He seemed to be getting upset, so the other boys kept quiet.

As the boys approached the house, Omi stood beside the barn on the south side, soaking up the sun in a dark coat. Mike led the way past the house and followed a path in the snow towards her. Each boy was in line, one behind the other.

"Hi, Omi. These are my friends I told you about," Mike said.

"*Aaniin*," she said in her native tongue, but she caught herself as before and corrected. "Hello," she said in a sweet tone and smile. "I am used to being on the reservation, I guess."

The boys were a bit shy, but Levi, trying to show off, said, "*Boozhoo niij.*"

Omi laughed, as did the others, and she quickly responded with, "Hello, friend."

"Where did you learn that, Levi?" Deevee asked.

Levi's comment helped break the ice, and before long, they were all in the barn looking over a wooden barricade used to keep six white rabbits from getting away. They were beautiful rabbits with long ears and fluffy tails. Old carrots and lettuce, gathered at the diner the day before, sat on a large tray in the corner. The rabbits absorbed the warmth from a lightbulb hanging from an old, gray extension cord; it was just enough to keep the water from freezing overnight. It seemed much warmer in the barn, and even warmer still after Omi closed the door and turned on the main lights. The boys sat down on some boxes and waited quietly.

Omi unexpectedly spoke, "I know you all have come to help me look for my lost rabbits, but it is good that we do not look. They are not here. There is nowhere else to look. They are gone. I fear an animal may have found them, and I do not want to find any remains if that is true." A few tears welled up in her eyes, and the boys looked down in respect. Eventually, Mike drew close to her and asked if there was anything they could do.

"How did your rabbits get out?" Gus asked. Mike looked at him rather harshly, but Omi touched his arm and assured him the question was okay.

"I had them all in these cages along the wall, but somehow the door to one of them was found opened this morning, and it was gone. I know I latched it closed. I just don't know how . . . the same thing happened yesterday morning, too."

"What time did you find it missing?" Gus asked.

"After the sunrise. The snow came last night, so I wanted to check on my rabbits early," she said.

"Did you check for animal tracks in the snow?" Levi asked.

"I had already been around the barn many times before I thought of it, so I did not," Omi answered. "But, on Friday, we moved these boxes from our home on the reservation. My mother backed her truck up to the door. On Saturday morning, I found my first rabbit missing, so maybe we hit the cage with a box. We've been looking for it all over town," she said.

The friends eventually gathered outside to look around. They turned up their collars again. There were a few other homes and buildings to the west of the house, but there were only fields to the north. The Anderson place was out of town at one time, but now it was nearly closed in by other homes, except on the one side. The house had a large lot—a farmyard at one time—and it was perfect for a girl and her pets.

"I'm sure you know a lot about rabbits, Omi. Do you want to help me find a blue one?" Mike blurted it out before he knew what he said. Surprise painted the faces of the other boys. Gus grabbed his arm and turned him around. He dragged him away from the others and whispered in his ear.

"If you tell her about the nest, I'm gonna—"

Gus was interrupted. "A blue rabbit? Mike, did you say blue rabbit?" Omi asked, her eyes widened.

Gus let him go and hoped Mike got the message. He stood quietly as Mike told the story of the blue rabbits in Gunder's glade and how it all got started. The story went on for several minutes, and Deevee and Levi asked to go back into the barn and out of the wind. They sat on the boxes, and Omi listened intently. She was instantly taken by Mike's story. By the expression on her face, she wanted to find a blue rabbit more than Mike did.

"I will go with you today," she said.

"It's too cold today," Mike said. "Let's see if it warms tomorrow."

"You come get me; I will go with you all," she said. "I will go with you all to find the blue rabbit."

CHAPTER FOUR

A Surprise in the Diner

As Monday began, school was out for Christmas break. There would be no school through the holidays and into January. The boys were free, and Mike had not forgotten about his plans to seek out a blue rabbit, but more importantly, he was going to spend time with Omi. He couldn't think of a better start to Christmas vacation. He readied himself with warm winter gear, "layering up" as his uncle Clair would say. Gus was not as thrilled, and Mike told him he could stay in bed if he wanted.

"Clair, have you seen Gunder lately?" Mike asked as he passed through the Cenex station on his way to the diner.

"No, I haven't seen him since Saturday. I hope you're not going to bother him, Mike," he said.

"Oh, no, I don't have to see him to look for blue rabbits."

As they talked, the side door of the station opened, and Bern Ebner walked in. He stood quietly for a moment then sat on the bench by the window. He appeared to be in no hurry to pay for his fuel, so he listened as the conversation continued.

"Mike! Really? Are you seriously going to look for blue rabbits? You know Gunder is probably seein' those gray jackrabbits. If you start working him up over this, he'll be in here every day talking about it. He's getting older, too. I don't think his little heart can take anymore, and I don't think mine can either," Clair said.

"I thought you believed Gunder."

"Oh, I do believe, just not all of it," Clair stated.

"He offered me his BB gun if I could get one, and I gotta try. He must be see'n something to be so scared. But like I said, I don't have to talk to him until I find one of those blue rabbits," Mike said as he headed out the door.

Clair offered one last bit of advice, even though he wasn't sure he should, "Try Gunder's glade, the clearing in the Christmas tree grove. He always called it a glade. He said that's where the rabbits ate the young saplings."

"Thanks, Uncle Clair, I will."

"Mike!" Clair yelled from the door, "You be careful out there, and take somebody with you. I don't want you by yourself. You hear?"

Mike offered a wave for understanding and turned toward the diner a few doors up. He knew Deevee and Levi would be there since the red Farmall tractor sat parked on the street, the long, wooded toboggan still tied to the hitch. He entered the diner and was greeted by several friends and their families having breakfast, and he chatted for a bit before drawing his attention to Deevee and Levi.

The boys motioned for him with a sense of urgency in their actions. Mike hurried over to the counter where they were folding cloth napkins for their mother. "Mike, you will not believe what we just heard from that family over there!" Deevee said with tremendous glee in his voice. Levi began talking, but Deevee cut him off. "I'll tell him; I'm the one who first heard it," he scolded.

"What did you hear, guys?" Mike asked.

"That family with the little girl were laughing and talking about seeing a blue rabbit crossing the road on their way into town this morning," Deevee explained.

"What?" Mike yelled loudly with unbelief.

"I know, we can't believe it. We couldn't wait for you to get here." The brothers began to laugh at their own news. "Go over there and find out where it was," they ordered.

"I can't go talk to them. I don't know that family," Mike explained.

"We have to know where it was seen. I thought you were the big rabbit detective, Mike," Levi said.

"No, you said that, not me," he quipped.

"You still have to go ask. You want that new BB gun, don't you?" Deevee asked.

"You're right. I really do want Gunder's pop gun," Mike answered with a certain sparkle in his eye. "Let's go! Can you leave with me now? I would really like to catch a ride on the toboggan out there."

"Aren't you forgetting something, Mike? Now go over there and ask that man where they were this morning," Deevee pointed as he spoke.

"Okay, give me a second," Mike said slowly.

Deevee asked him to wait for a minute before he walked away. He returned with a cup of hot chocolate and handed it to Mike. "Take a sip of this real quick; it'll give you the nerve." Levi laughed out loud at the thought as Mike sipped. He drank until it was half empty then put it down and slowly walked over to the gentleman and his family.

"Sir, might I ask you a question?" The man nodded at him. "I heard you saw a rabbit this morning on your way into town. Was it really blue? My friends heard you tell of it earlier."

The man smiled but pointed at his daughter. She was about five or six years old and was chewing on a mouthful of pancakes. Her mother excused her for a moment with a hand on her back and then asked her to tell the story of the blue rabbit she saw, but only after her mouth was clear.

"I sawed a bunny rabbit on the road by the Christmas trees. I think it was blue, 'cause I sawed it jump off the road and runned away. I sawed it out my window, but daddy didn't see it. I think mommy sawed it, too," she said.

Mike smiled at her with respect. She was adorable, but he wasn't sure he could believe her. He turned his attention to her mother. "Ma'am did you really see it?"

"Young man, I don't want to say I did, because who wants to sound foolish, but I'm pretty sure that rabbit was blue," she said.

"Sir," Mike began to ask, "where abouts was it?"

"It's like she said, by the Christmas trees out on the East and West, coming into town.

Mike knew that the residents of Willow City used the name East and West to describe the road passing by Gunder's farm. The Christmas trees were probably in reference to the many spruce trees planted along the road and around Gunder's farm; there were many acres of trees, and they stood out along the road which traveled through mostly farmland. He thanked them for the news and tried to leave.

"Son, why did you want to know?" the man asked.

"Oh, um, well, we just thought it was a fun story; maybe we'll try to catch one," Mike said with a laugh. As he left, he heard the young girl say how she wanted a blue rabbit. "I would love one," he whispered to himself.

He walked back to Deevee and Levi, who were putting on their coats. He grabbed his hot chocolate and turned the bottom up, pouring it down his throat. "We better go now. We have a real mystery on our hands," he said with an ominous tone. Deevee and Levi nodded their heads in agreement. "Gunder may be telling the truth, and what if this jinx thing is catchy?" Mike asked with wide eyes. "One of us could—well you know."

"Die?" Levi asked.

"Well, you never know," Mike answered.

The boys turned up their collars and expected a cold blast of winter air as they left out the diner's front door, but instead they encountered the tall German farmer with unusually dirty hands. Mike's ominous tone earlier in the diner was realized as the words from Bern Ebner poured down their necks like the cold winter air.

"You boys, here," he said angrily. It caught the boys off guard, and it seemed to come out of nowhere. "I heard you boyz is bozerin' Gunder out on zee East und Vest. You leaf zat old man alone. He's crazy."

Deevee and Levi knew they couldn't say a word. He was a good customer for the diner, and their mother would be very upset if they disrespected him. But hanging around Gus for so many years seemed to be rubbing off on Mike, and he wanted to know why he couldn't make an effort toward a new BB gun.

"Sir?" he asked in a confused sounding way. "There's no harm in hunting rabbits."

"Vhat hares you be huntin'?" he asked quickly.

"Blue rabbits, sir. Some people have seen a blue rabbit, and Gunder don't like 'em," Mike returned.

"You're vasting your time, boy. Zere ain't no blue hares. Now, get out of my vay." He took hold of the diner's door and swung it open. He turned one last time, and with an angry look on his face and an angrier tone in his voice, he spoke an unfamiliar phrase to the boys, "Es geht dich nichts an."

A woman coming through the door interrupted him and set him back on his heels. "Mr. Ebner! Zose are yust boys!" the woman scolded as she walked out the door. "Get in zee auto und take me to zee house! I am ashamed of you!" she said harshly.

Mike and the boys were dumbfounded and looked at each other in shock. Bern walked a few steps down the street and climbed into an old truck. Mike quickly regained his sensibilities and called out to the woman.

"Ma'am, do you know what he said to us?"

"Oh, I'm zorry, boys. My husband is a bit cranky today. I told him to vatch his mouth; no harm. He's here to pick me up."

"But what did he say to us?" Mike asked again.

"Vell, he vas a little rude. He zaid, *It's none of your buziness.* I'm fery zorry. Good day to you."

The boys were just as confused as before but continued walking towards the tractor. Deevee climbed into the driver's seat and started it. He could see the German couple in the truck arguing, and he tried not to look. Mike and Levi were stretching out the rope and the toboggan for the ride down the snow-covered street to Omi's house.

Suddenly, a man from the grocery store ran out towards Bern's truck.

"Bern!" he called. "Don't leave. I got your order. Let me get it for you."

The boys took interest without drawing attention to themselves, and eventually, the man brought out a large box of red cabbage.

Bern jumped out of his truck, grabbed the box from the man, and threw it in the bed of his pickup. He left quickly, turning north for home.

"How much red cabbage does he eat?" Levi asked with a chuckle. "That's a lot of red cabbage."

"Mom says Germans love cabbage, especially at Christmas time," Deevee explained.

It was a short ride to Omi's house. Mike and Levi were covered with snow by the time they arrived, and the boys found her eager to go on a hunt for blue rabbits.

Because of the many fences separating Omi's property to the roads on the north side, the boys drove the tractor around the edge of town and then north to the East and West. Deevee and Levi sat on the bench seat of the tractor, and Omi sat behind Mike on the toboggan hanging on as they occasionally hit large snow drifts along the edge of the road. They traveled a mile west to Gunder's place and stopped at the edge of the spruce trees surrounding his farmstead. There were thousands of trees planted in huge arc formations around Gunder's home. Row after row ran north, then gradually turned west, then south to meet the road once more. The trees along the outer edge were much older than the ones closer towards the middle. A few smaller trees looked as if they had replaced larger trees years ago when Gunder's family sold the trees during the Christmas season. It was nearly an eighth of a mile from the east side of Gunder's trees to the west side. Seeing the situation as it was, Deevee shut off the tractor so they could talk.

"The blue rabbits could be anywhere in those trees. I guess I didn't realize how many trees he had. When you're in the truck, it doesn't seem so big." Mike sulked as he stood and shook the snow off of his coat. He brushed Omi's coat and knocked a large snow pile off the top of her hat.

"Where is the glade, Mike? You know, the one Gus told us about? Wouldn't that be the best place to start?" Deevee asked.

"Yeah! Great idea, Deevee. Gus said it was be-hind his house, but I'll bet we'll have to walk a long way through deep snow. Look at the snow drifts in there," Mike said.

The roads running east and west were always less snow-covered than the roads north and south. Westerly winds blew snow across the roads, and any obstruction swirled the wind and caused the snow to drop and pile. Snow fences erected some distance from the roads helped catch the snow be-fore it could cover them. But evergreen trees did the same thing, and the snow was deep around the rows of trees. Mike knew it would be worse for him due to his shorter legs. Snow might fall lightly, but even an inch of snow could cause large drifts in the presence of wind.

Levi evaluated the situation. "We can follow the trees along the middle rows; there will be less snow there. It should lead us right to the glade if it's in the middle of the rows."

"Okay, jump on; I'll park the tractor off the road at the end of his driveway," Deevee said.

.

CHAPTER FIVE

THE BLUE RABBIT STAKEOUT

Omi followed the boys into the rows of pines. The snow was deep, but it wasn't as bad as they had imagined. They trudged through the snow and along the middle rows of pines for nearly three hundred yards. The sun's location in the sky proved they were turning west, yet a glade had not come into view. Omi pointed out many tree stumps from cut trees over the years, and she stated that with every stump there seemed to be a new tree planted close to it. "Gunder tried hard to keep trees growing," Levi said.

"There are a lot of little trees growing here, too. Looks like they're planting themselves. This place is turning into an evergreen forest," Mike added.

Mike noticed large hollow pockets under some of the bigger trees where wind had made perfect circular rooms out of snow. The wind blew round and round, dumping the snow into walls around the base of the trees. Under some trees, the ground was still visible. Omi detected something on the base of one tree.

"Hey, guys. Look at the bite marks on this tree. I think a rabbit's been chewing on it," she exclaimed.

Omi fell to all fours and looked down under the branches. "Yes, that's from a rabbit for sure."

"You better get a closer look, Omi," Mike said as he nudged her into the tree hollow with his boot.

She tumbled down in and rolled on her back as the other boys pulled Mike in, too. They laughed hard at each other, and they sat down to rest. They had made a new friend in Omi; she fit in so well.

"You're okay, Omi, but you better get him back for that," Deevee said.

"I'm a Chippewa, and I'll sneak up on him someday and scare the feathers off of him." She laughed.

Unexpectedly, Levi quickly put his hands up and motioned them downward. "Stay down everybody," he whispered. "Look over there." He pointed.

Their heads popped up just enough to clear the snowy edge, and each positioned themselves to see through the boughs of pine. In the distance, past several tree rows, two legs could be seen tromping through the snow. The branches were too low to make out who it was, but it wasn't long before Mike knew.

BOOM! A loud crack of gunfire went off, and the sound of lead shot could be heard ripping through the trees. The legs moved westward out of sight. Mike looked at them all "He must be seein' things again. He's got that old 10-gauge, and he's scare'n critters away."

"Didn't you say something to me about him not seein' well?" Levi asked.

"Yeah."

"Well, he might think we're critters if we don't let him know we're here," Levi said.

"Yeah, we might go home heavier than when we came. That's what our dad always says," Deevee said.

The others laughed and discussed the issues for some time. Omi finally had the best plan for seeing their way clear. "If he thinks he's seeing blue rabbits, then he'll head into the glade where he said he saw one. My grandfather says to always hunt first where you know game comes. It's a joke in my family."

"We can follow his tracks if we're quiet," Mike said. With that, the group crawled out of the tree hollow through the snow and made their way to the path Gunder took. The tracks were very clear, but they seemed to be heading left toward the farmstead.

Suddenly, Gunder yelled behind them in a loud and scary voice. He had quickly circled around and behind them. "You stop right dare. Who are you and vhy are you in my juletres?"

Mike yelled loudly in self-defense, "Gunder, it's me, Mike. You asked me to find the blue rabbits for you!"

"Oh, my!" he said. "Mike, you come here now. Come close, vill you?" he said. "I tought I hert someting out dare." Mike and the others came trudging through the snow toward him.

"You really scared us, Gunder."

"Ya, and you really scare Gunder, too. Have you seen da blue hare? Get dem all, vill you?" he asked.

Reaching Gunder, Omi caught his eye. She waited for him to say something but couldn't assume what it would be. "Tell me your friends, Mike. Dese all here to help catch da hare?" Gunder asked.

Mike introduced his friends to Gunder, and he was impressed that so many wanted to help. He eventually stated his need to go home but cautioned Mike to always let him know if he was on his property. Mike agreed and told him Deevee's tractor was in his drive. As Gunder turned to leave, he heard his name again. "Um, Gunder? The glade, the place where the blue rabbits were seen. Which way is it?"

"Oh, yes. Not far. Go back to da middle rows and valk fifty yarts more. You vill see it fine. I vill let you be. You get dose hare, vill you? You get dem all. Do vhat you vill. Good luck." He mumbled a few more words that were not understood, and then turned and continued mumbling as he disappeared into the trees, but the boys and Omi clearly heard an unmistakable laughter, too.

Deevee, Levi, and Omi looked a bit unsure, and Mike sensed it. "Oh, he's just a crazy old man, guys; don't pay him any mind. I'll get word to him next time we're here." But Omi didn't appreciate Gunder's lack of respect for the rabbits. She didn't want harm to come to a blue rabbit, and she made herself clear on the issue.

"I can't believe an old man would think a rabbit harmed his family. He better not harm any rabbits I see, especially a blue one," she said and folded her arms as tight as her winter wear would allow.

The group began their trudging walk again and eventually stumbled into the glade. It was a beautiful winter wonderland with tall trees looming all around the perimeter. There was only a slight breeze present, and the sky was as blue as the rabbit they were looking for. The dark pines closed in the glade with peacefulness, and the white snow on their upper boughs bent them into submission. Tall grasses still poked up through the fluffy snow, and the slightest waft of air made them wiggle as if tempting the rabbits to take a bite. But there were no rabbit tracks there, and Mike made known his disappointment. "This place is perfect for a jackrabbit. I guess Gunder's done a good job runnin' 'em off."

Omi tried to turn his disappointment around. "We can stake it out, like on T.V. I'm sure we'll see something come along if we're quiet."

"You watch T.V.?" Levi asked her.

"Oh, I love to watch that new show *Gunsmoke*. We had a T.V. in the community center on the reservation," she said.

"That's my favorite, too," Mike said. "Yeah, let's sit and wait a bit. If we don't see anything, we can move toward the highway."

"Oh, no! Mike, you don't have your BB gun," Deevee said sadly.

"I can't use that old thing; plus, we're only here to do just what we're doin', a stakeout. If we see a blue rabbit, we'll come back and set a trap. I decided I didn't want to hurt a blue rabbit, for more than one reason."

Levi leaned into Deevee and whispered, "Yeah, he wants Omi to have one, that's why."

"I heard that," Mike said as he threw a snowball at him.

"It's true; I don't want him to hurt it. We're going to catch it," Omi said in a sweet tone. "I'm going to have a blue rabbit, I hope."

They wandered back to the edge of the glade and found a shallow tree hollow, jumped inside, and made themselves comfortable. Watching in all directions for some time they saw only a hawk circling the same ground they occupied.

"Rabbits don't like hawks. We might as well go on home," Mike said. "We'll try again tomorrow."

"Wait!" Omi said in a loud excited voice. "I think I know why that little girl saw a blue rabbit on the road. What was across the road from Gunder's drive?"

"If I remember, there were some shrubs and bushes off in the ditch," he answered.

"Shrubs and bush twigs are a rabbit's favorite food in the winter. I'll bet that's where we'll find one, and we can still stay in the pine trees for cover as we look across the road," she said.

"Sounds logical to me," Levi said. Mike agreed.

"I'm hungry anyway. Let's go back into town first," Deevee said.

"Hungry? It's only been a few hours," Mike said.

But the rest agreed with Deevee. The hard walk through the snow and trying to stay warm used a lot of their energy. The boys looked at each other all bundled up; mittens, hats, and pull-over rubber boots made them all look so funny, and they laughed at each other. Their collars were turned up with a wide crocheted scarf wrapped nearly three times around their throats, each one of a different color. Omi was the only one who looked warm in her fur coat. Her mittens were handmade from deer hide, and they had special embroidered wrist collars that traveled nearly halfway to her elbows. Her coat had a large roomy hood with a coyote's tail fur sewn to the front which nearly hid her face when the wind blew, but Omi didn't wear her hood much due to her long black hair, which helped keep her warm. It reminded Mike of the Inuit who lived far north in the Arctic.

The boys and Omi pushed each other around in laughter and then made their way out of the tree hollow. They decided to take the shortest route back to the tractor and turned straight south. After a few minutes of snow trudging, they were surprised to find themselves between Gunder's house and the barn. The tractor could be seen at the end of the drive. Mike and Omi began holding each other back as they walked a little faster. Mike had every intention of riding on the tractor, not behind it. Omi understood this, too, and she pulled on his arm as they began a sprint. Deevee and Levi knew a seat on the tractor was up for grabs. Playing along, they began to run. It was a long trip down the drive with heavy winter coats, hats, and boots, and each looked even funnier as they ran. Deevee's long legs brought him in first, and he climbed up onto the tractor with Omi on his heels.

Levi and Mike complained about Deevee's long legs, but they were impressed with Omi's speed. She was of average height, but her limbs were long and thin, and her stride would make any sport's coach wish her on a team. Still, they would have to ride the toboggan back to Willow City, so they began stretching their scarves over their faces and pulling down on their hats. But the tractor would not start.

"What's wrong, Deevee?" Levi called.

"It's cold, and the battery's dead. It just won't start. I think we'll have to walk," he answered.

"Walk?" cried Mike. He waited for a response but didn't receive one. After a short pause, they still looked helpless. Mike knew what they were thinking, but none wanted to say it—ask Mr. Nilsen to help. Still unsure about Gunder, Deevee looked back at Levi and shrugged. Mike caught the gesture and intervened. "I'll go ask. Don't worry, it'll be fine."

"We can take a shortcut through the fields, boys," Omi suggested. "We only went the long way around because of the fences. If we walk southeast, we'll be just a little west of my house. I'll bet it's less than two miles."

"I'd rather walk than to talk to Mr. Nilsen again," Levi said. "He's seems very strange to me."

"That's fine by me. More time on the hunt. Maybe we'll scare one up in the fields like I was doin' the other day," Mike touted. "That's a big field." He was looking off into the southeast. There seemed to be no end to it.

Deevee and Omi jumped off the tractor and joined the others heading across the graveled road. They stepped down into the ditch and up the other side, through some heavy snow drifts and brush, and onto a stubble wheat field. Omi was in the lead, and she had taken them through an opening in the bushes lining the field that was mentioned earlier. The brush was much higher than it looked from the other side of the road. Omi quietly pointed out a few old animal tracks that were running in and out of the thick brush. Mike nodded his approval with a smile as they walked into the open field, but he stopped and addressed the other boys. "I know we'll scare up a rabbit in this. Let's walk along these shrubs for a bit; there's tracks all over here," he said excitedly.

The snow wasn't deep out in the open field, but close to the shrubs on the south side, the snow had piled up. The drifts left crests and valleys of snow strewn out thirty feet or so into the field then leveled out like ocean waves smoothing a sandy beach. The four walked along slowly peeking into the brush where tracks could be seen, but no rabbits were found.

Eventually, Mike began thinking about his last walk through a field and turned his attention to the one he was on. The field was very similar; the cut wheat stalks were not as tall as the sunflower stalks, but they were still visible, and black dirt patches were visible in places where the snow had blown clear. It would be hard to see a hunkering rabbit with so many shadows and color variations. Mike didn't have the advantage of the raised ground of the railroad tracks as before, so he offered up a plan for the group.

"I guess we better go now. But if we have to walk through this field, then I think we should spread out. I'm sure we'll scare up a rabbit with four of us walking. Stay about fifty feet from each other," he suggested.

"Let's just get back to town as fast as we can. I'm hungry, and my feet are getting cold," Deevee grumbled. "I hope your uncle will give the tractor a boost."

"That's what he does, but you might have to pay a little for the service call." Mike laughed.

Forming a straight line, they began walking southeastward. They fanned out quickly, staying vigilant as they tripped over frozen clumps of dirt, stubble, and mini snow drift shifting in endless positions along the ground. Gunder's farm got smaller as they walked, and soon, only the tall pines stood to mark where they had been. Deevee and Levi were to Mike's right, and Omi walked on his left. Slowly the fifty foot distance between Mike and Omi closed.

"Fifty feet apart, you two!" Levi yelled. Deevee laughed out loud just before he was hit with a snowball.

"Mind your business. You're supposed to be looking for rabbits, not watching me," Mike yelled back. Omi put her head down shyly as she disappeared into her furry hood.

Suddenly, a jackrabbit sprang up to Levi's left. It startled everyone. It was extremely fast, but Mike took off in pursuit. The others followed, yelling and screaming their support and laughing as they ran. "Get 'em Mike! Get 'em!" But Mike could not.

He stopped eventually and fell into a small drift of snow onto his back, panting heavily. As Omi and the boys arrived, they joined him in the snow. They lay for minutes, catching their breath.

"A trap sounds like a good plan," Deevee said. "You'll never catch one running."

Their attention was taken just long enough to miss a large Oliver tractor coming up from behind them. It scared them all as they sat up in attention then slowly stood to watch its arrival. It was snorting black soot and throwing dirt and snow from its tires, and its loader bucket was moving up and down in a menacing way. The driver had a foul look on his face, and it wasn't long before they knew who it was. The tractor stopped in front of them, but the engine remained revving. Omi moved herself behind Mike, and he straightened his back to stand taller.

The showdown finally ended as the tractor shut down. Bern Ebner climbed off the tractor and walked toward them. "I zink I'll ask vy you're on my field? You're looking for zoze blue hares, und you're on my property. I told you to leaf it alone, und look, here you schtand!"

"We're just crossing it to get back to Willow City. Our tractor won't start, so we had to walk home," Mike tried to explain.

"I don't vant to hear your excuzes! You're gonna give zat old man a heart attack talkin' up zoze blue hares. Leaf it be, und leaf him alone, und get off my field!" He was angry, and he kicked some snow and dirt on his last word. "Vell?"

Omi stepped out from behind Mike. "Why do you care if we look for blue rabbits to help an old man?"

"Nones of your buziness, young man!" he said sharply.

"I'm a girl!" she said as she removed her furry hood.

"Vell, so I see. No vonder you vant a fluffy little bunny hare," he said rudely.

Being the oldest and tallest, Deevee stepped up and tried to smooth everything over. "The fastest way off your property is south, so we'll just get walkin'. Come on guys."

"You're not valking any furzer on my property. You're gonna get in zat loader bucket, und I'll be takin' you to zee south fence. Zat's vhat you're gonna do," he ordered.

Living in a farming community, the middle schoolers had ridden in a tractor bucket many times. Deevee and Levi many more. But they did not trust Bern.

"That's not a good idea. I think we'll just walk," Deevee said.

"No, wait. We'll get in, but you take us all the way to the Cenex station in town," Mike said.

"Fine, cauze you're getting off my property right now, zo get in!" Bern yelled.

Bern climbed into the driver's seat and started the tractor. He revved it up and black soot streamed once again from the stack. He lowered the bucket, and the group stepped in. They sat tightly together as he lifted them high over the tractor. The bumpy field nearly bounced them silly as he sped forward, and Bern seemed to be hitting every lump and drift he could. Side to side they slid, and up and down they bounced as the tractor rocked over the field. It wasn't long before they realized he was not heading to the road, but they could not get off. He continued south and finally arrived at a barbed wire fence on the south line of his property. Bern hung the bucket far over the fence and slowly began dumping it forward.

"Hey! Stop!" Mike yelled. "Let us down, you sodbuster!" But it was too late. They were dumped out from six feet up and piled on top of each other as they came to a sudden stop.

Bern began laughing as he reversed his tractor. "Und schtay off!" he yelled.

CHAPTER SIX

A Trail to the Barn

Deevee and Levi had been dumped from a loader tractor before, but it was always into a pile of hay on the ranch. Their father loved to see the boys have fun during the long summers when hay was being cut. But the boys and Omi were a long way from summer as they untied themselves from a giant leg and arm knot in the snow. "That was extremely mean of that man!" Omi protested.

"Are you okay, Omi?" Mike asked as he stood and brushed the snow off his body.

"I guess so," she said. "The weeds under this fence caught the snow. I'm glad it was a soft landing.

"Well, I'm not okay!" Levi complained. "I'm gonna flatten his tires the next time he comes into town. You just watch; I'm gonna do it. Maybe he'll drive that snortin' tractor into town, and I'll set a few nails for him."

"You'll do no such thing, Levi," Deevee said in a fatherly tone. "Now, is everybody really okay?"

Each one nodded a head as they beat the snow off each other. Taking the lead, Omi began walking east along the fence, staying off of the snow drift area. The boys followed.

"Just a little farther, boys. We're just a little north of town," Omi said. Suddenly, she stopped and remained motionless for a few moments. "Look at this! This trail seems to lead toward my house. Look, it's through there."

The boys looked down her arm as she pointed through a gap in a few trees and past a couple of distant sheds. They were nearing town, and Omi's house wasn't far. The trail was in the snow, and it looked as though several trips had been made coming and going. The footprints were large but undefined in the snow. Some were older and covered with recent snow, but others looked fresher to Omi.

"The trail has been used not so long ago. We can walk it, too. We'll go to my house first. My mother can drive us to the station to see your uncle, Mike."

"Maybe Gunder comes this way into town when it's cold. It is shorter than the East and West," Deevee suggested.

"I haven't seen him, but I just moved into that house a few days ago," Omi said. "Maybe he does walk this way. But we better get going."

Eventually, the trail headed toward town and branched off in several different directions. Levi guessed hunters, sportsman, or people on nature hikes were using the trails to get out of town. The branch they were on led in the direction Omi's house. But, as the trail reached Omi's street, numerous tracks in the snow feathered off in every direction; it was clear that most were made by Omi's family previously looking for her rabbits, but some were larger than any her family would leave.

The boys briefly stopped for a look at Omi's rabbits. She was glad to see them all safe and warm. They decided to walk the few blocks more and made plans to pick her up on the way back to Gunder's farm. They left for the Cenex station to find Mike's uncle, Clair. Despite his short legs, Mike led the group down Main Street's sidewalk; he had a sense of urgency about him. Having to walk past the Iceberg Diner, Deevee and Levi noticed a number of cars parked on the street, and they peeked in the door to see what their mother was doing. The diner was packed with many of the farmers from around the area for someone's birthday party. Mike ran back to the boys and grabbed them. "What's wrong with you guys? You wanna wash dishes? If your mother sees you, that's what you'll be doin', and you have to ask my uncle for help with your tractor, not me. Let's go! You can get something to eat after we get that tractor runnin'."

Clair was not in sight, but they found Gus sitting inside the station. The news about Bern Ebner was quickly shared. It riled him, and he stated his disappointment about letting Mike go without him.

"If I would've been there, old Bern wouldn't have done that. He knows who I am: *Clair's son*. He buys gas here for his equipment, and dad could run him off if he wanted to."

Mike reassured him. "It's okay, Gus, nobody got hurt, and we learned a few things out there today."

"Yeah, Mike loves Omi!" Levi laughed.

"Knock it off. She's just a new friend, and we have things in common," Mike returned.

"Did you see a blue rabbit?" Gus asked.

"No, but we found Gunder's glade in the pine trees. We even found Gunder there," Mike said.

"We did run after a rabbit, though," Deevee said. "Never even got close."

Mike finally asked the question that they had wanted to ask for a couple of miles. "Is your dad here? Deevee's Farmall tractor won't start."

"He's at the diner eatin'. You walked right passed it."

"I guess we'll go back," Levi said. "Mom can fix us something to eat. I just hope she doesn't ask us to do the dishes."

"Yeah, I'm hungry!" Deevee said. "Whose birthday is it, Gus?"

"Oh, it's Melvin Hanson's birthday, I think, but the party should be over by now," Gus said.

"Good, 'cause I'm gonna grab the leftovers, and mom always makes chocolate cake. Let's go, Levi," Deevee called as he sailed out the door.

"Tell my dad to come back. I want some, too," Gus said with a worried look.

The boys took off for the diner but promised to come back with Clair and a piece of cake. They ran into the diner and found Clair in their favorite corner booth. Deevee swallowed hard and asked the question. "Clair, could I ask your help with my tractor? The battery died out at Gunder's farm, and we can't get it started."

"How did you get back?" he asked sipping his last bit of coffee.

Mike jumped into the conversation. "We walked all the way back, Uncle Clair."

"Wow, that's a long walk, boys. Wait!" he interjected. "So you really did go out there looking for blue rabbits?"

"Yes, but you told me not to bother Gunder, so we came all the way back to ask you."

"Oh, really, I guess I'm the lucky one today," Clair said. Other men sitting in the booth laughed along with Clair.

"My boys do the same thing to me. Fix this, fix that," one farmer said.

"Deevee, I'd help you, but I think you better just ask your own dad. He's right over there." Clair pointed.

Deevee's father was sitting by the front window with his back to the door. The boys hadn't noticed him with the crowd in the room. He was in a serious conversation with a man in a business suit. The boys thanked Clair and walked toward their father; Mike followed. They were respectful and let their father finish speaking before they interrupted.

"Sir, I don't know what to tell you. My horses need the land for grazing; I have a ranch, no land, no ranch, and the other quarter belongs to my wife's family. That 160 acres isn't for sale. I'll need every acre if I buy cows this spring. I just can't part with any land right now," Deevee and Levi's father said.

"I appreciate your time, Mr. Wagner. I'll let my client know. Good day." The man stood, nodded his head at their father, and left.

"Dad, what are you doing in town today?" Dee-vee asked.

Mr. Wagner, surprised to see his boys, grabbed them and pulled them close. "What are you boys doin'?" he asked as he tickled their ribs. "Hi there, Mikey."

"Dad, the tractor won't start, and it's out at Gunder Nilsen's farm. We walked all the way into town for help. Can you get it started for us?"

"Well, why didn't you ask Gunder for a start? He has tractors," Mr. Wagner said.

"My father didn't want me to bother him, sir," Mike added suddenly.

"Were you at his house, or did you break down on the road out there?" Mr. Wagner asked.

Mike spoke up again so Deevee did not give anything away. He feared Mr. Wagner would forbid his boys to be over there, and Mike needed the boys to help find the blue rabbits. From what Deevee said in the nest, Mike would have to be careful with his explanation.

"Deevee and Levi were nice enough to drop me and Omi off at Gunder's farm." He dropped the name Omi and hoped it would lead the conversation away from blue rabbits. "He turned the tractor off, but it wouldn't start again."

"Oh, okay, I see. Well, I guess we better get out there and get it. I wouldn't want it damaged by those blue rabbits," Mr. Wagner replied.

"What did you say, Dad?" Levi asked as the others stood motionless.

"Yes, that's right. I know you were out there looking for blue rabbits. Clair told me he thought that's where you were this morning. Ya' know, Deevee, I seem to remember telling you not to get around old Gunder. He can be a little strange sometimes. Nice try, Mike, but your cover's blown," Mr. Wagner said. Mike hung his head and mumbled an apology.

"Dad, what did the man in the suit want from you?" Deevee asked to change the subject.

"He wanted me to sell my land to his client, one of our neighbors."

"Who wants our land, Dad?"

"Bern Ebner wants to expand, and he seems to think that planting more crop this spring will be his saving grace. The almanac calls for a bumper crop in our area this coming year. He wants to plant wheat and corn on it. The bank cleared him for a big loan, but I don't think he'll find any land nearby.

"Bern Ebner wants our land?" Levi asked.

"Oh, yes. He's asked every neighbor around him for more land, but nobody's selling," Mr. Wagner said. "He is one angry man, and he refuses to rent the land. He wants to own it. One fellow told me he won't even talk to him anymore."

The boys didn't want to worry their father, so they didn't share the interactions they'd had with Bern. They couldn't imagine Bern sharing it, either, especially since he had been so rude to them. If their father wanted to, he could keep them away from everybody if he feared harm would come of it. To add to their decision, Mike was nudging them toward the door, but before they left their father's side, Deevee asked the question one last time. "Dad, will you help us?"

Mr. Wagner finally gave in since it was his tractor in question. He waited on the boys as they gathered a quick snack and some chocolate cake. They rolled up a large piece in a napkin and headed out the door.

They ran ahead of Mr. Wagner to deliver Gus's cake then piled into the pickup truck on top of each other. Mike talked Mr. Wagner into driving past his house to pick up a trap. Mike had gathered an old wooden box, some string, and a stick sharpened on both ends. He threw it in the back of the truck, and they were off. One more stop collected Omi, but they had to wait as she laced up her boots and leggings, fed her rabbits, and donned her thick parka. After several honks of the horn, she jumped into the truck on top of three laughing boys who didn't think there was room for one more. "Took you long enough," Mike said in jest.

They arrived at Gunder's farm and found the tractor as they had left it. Mr. Wagner gathered some cables to hook to the battery, raised the hood on his truck, and walked toward the Farmall Cub tractor. He unscrewed the wing nuts from the battery box lid under the seat. "Well, there's your problem, boys; your battery cables have been disconnected," Mr. Wagner said with surprise. "I know those were tightly installed because I put this battery in here myself."

"Dad, how can that be?" Deevee asked.

"Somebody's been in here today; look at the dirt rubbed off on the side of the box. I didn't do that. Did you mess with the battery today, son?" he asked.

"No, Dad. Levi, were you lookin' at the battery?" Deevee asked.

"Nope."

Omi jumped in. "I know who did it; that mean old man, Bern, did it—"

Mike grabbed her before she said too much, but it didn't change what Mr. Wagner said next.

"I guess his reputation is getting around; even the new girl knows about angry Mr. Ebner. What did he do to you, sweetheart?"

Omi understood the message Mike was sending by his apparent hushing, and she quickly covered the statement. "My mother doesn't like him much. He was rude to her in the hardware store. He grabbed the last paintbrush in front of my mother."

"Well, I can understand, I guess. Some people get a little strange when they're desperate," he said. "But I'm pretty sure Bern wouldn't have any reason to take your cables off. It must've been Gunder. I bet he came to look it over."

Mike knew differently, and from Omi's statement, she was sure it was Bern. She whispered to Mike behind Mr. Wagner's truck. "Bern saw the tractor, that's how he knew we were in the field. He knew we would have to walk home. He set us up."

"I think you're right, Omi, but we'll talk about it after Deevee's father leaves."

After reattaching the cable ends to the battery, Mr. Wagner screwed down the cover and started the tractor. Levi quickly called the passenger seat for the ride back to town.

Suddenly, a loud commotion was heard up the long drive toward Gunder's house.

"Da blue hare! Da blue hare! Get dat blue hare!"

Gunder was running faster than an old man should run, and he was carrying his 10-gauge. Mr. Wagner panicked and ran toward him. "Children, get behind the tractor now!" he screamed.

Mike quickly grabbed Omi and pulled her in with the others, but as fast as he did, Omi broke his grip and cried, "I see it! A blue rabbit! Look!"

Sitting in the middle of the road was a blue colored rabbit. By the looks on their faces, the boys could not believe what they were seeing. They didn't hear the arguing between Gunder and Mr. Wagner. Their senses were frozen as they looked upon the marvel. Quickly, Mike ran to the truck and grabbed his trap. Mr. Wagner had taken hold of Gunder and was holding him back.

"Gunder! Stop! You can't use that thing; there are children here." He and Gunder were dancing around and around with their hands on a skyward pointing 10-gauge. The commotion didn't deter Omi, and she jumped out from behind the tractor after it. Mike had his wooden box, stick, and string, and followed Omi out onto the road. Terrified, the rabbit bounded off into the ditch, up the other side, and into the thicket of brush and bushes that lined the large wheat field. The snow left perfect tracks to follow, but the brush was so thick they could not be followed.

"We got it now!" Mike screamed "I'll get you a blue rabbit, Omi, and I'm getting Gunder's pop gun!"

"I tolt you I see blue hare," Gunder called out loudly. "I seed someting from my vindow."

Mr. Wagner was still trying to calm him down and reassured him the kids would get the rabbit.

"Gunder, now don't scare it away for the boys. If you want it caught, you'll have to stay calm."

"My sveet Vigdis vould not be dead if it veren't for da blue hare."

Omi and the boys were now head deep in the brush looking for the rabbit, but it couldn't be found. Their scarves caught on the bush twigs and pulled on their necks. Mike knew it wouldn't run into the open field since the brush was so thick. The boys couldn't penetrate the thicket, and there were other dead grasses and weeds creating much cover for any rabbit. "It's under the grass; we'll never find it. I can't see a thing, Mike. Let's set the trap somewhere close," Omi said.

Mr. Wagner led Gunder to the side of the road and watched as they set their trap. The trap was set between the bushes along the edge of the field and far enough from the road. Mike knew that Bern would remove it if he saw it on his property. Omi watched carefully as Mike turned the box over and lifted one end. He had placed a small nail on the inside on the opposite end. The nail was bent over and formed a hook through which the string was run. He tied one end of the string to the sharpened stick. Clearing the snow, he placed the stick to hold up the end of the box and laid the other end of the string on the ground near the center of the box-covered area. "I just need some bait, Omi. I need something a rabbit won't refuse."

"Gunder, we need bait for the trap!" Omi yelled across the road.

Gunder put both hands in the air and turned toward the house. "I haf yust the right ting for you." He turned back for a moment, walked toward Mr. Wagner, smiled, and reached for his firearm. Mr. Wagner handed it back, but Gunder didn't notice the shells had been removed. They both laughed as Mr. Wagner held out his hand with the three missing shells. "Be right back; don't go avay," Gunder added in a happy tone.

Mr. Wagner walked across the road and made his way to the trap Mike had set. "How do you think that will work?" he asked.

Omi wasn't sure it would work, either. "How can a rabbit tip that over?" she asked.

"I'll put Gunder's bait under the box and tie it to the end of the string. When the rabbit tries to take it, it'll pull on the string. The string goes around that nail and back to the stick. I'll put the stick just right so the slightest movement makes it fall. I've caught squirrels and cats with it. I think I can catch a rabbit, too."

While waiting for Gunder, Mike spent the time looking for the blue rabbit. Deevee and Levi's father returned, and they helped him make some other adjustments to the tractor, then the boys were ready to leave. As Gunder came down the drive, Deevee turned the tractor around. "Gunder, did you try fixing the tractor while we were away this afternoon?" Deevee asked.

"I did not know you vere having trouble vith it."

"Somebody unhooked the battery cables while we were in the woods," Deevee returned.

"Vell, I vus in da woods vith you, too," Gunder replied.

Mr. Wagner looked at Deevee with question, but he said nothing. Deevee didn't want to discuss it any further so questions wouldn't be asked. "You two get back to the house so you can do your evening chores. Enough running around for one day," Mr. Wagner ordered.

Mike and Omi heard the statement as they walked out to meet Gunder. He had a large carrot in his hands. Omi took it from him, and the boys laughed at her. "Wow, that's a big carrot. Are you trying to catch a giant rabbit? Better get a bigger box!" Levi teased.

Mike tied the carrot to the string. He tightened the string through the nail loop and positioned the stick just right so the slightest movement would cause it to fall. He and Omi admired it then ran to the toboggan, pulling their hats and scarves over their faces.

Omi sat behind Mike on the toboggan and wrapped her arms around him. There were ropes lining the toboggan's edge, but she chose to hold onto Mike instead. Silently, she took one glove off for a short moment to reveal her fingers to Mike. They were crossed for good luck, and he nodded his head in approval. Mike crossed his fingers, too. Both were very excited at the prospects of having a blue rabbit in the trap by morning.

The evening seemed colder as they arrived back in town. Fearing an angry father and the lateness of the hour, Deevee dropped Mike and Omi off on Main Street and headed for the ranch with Levi next to him. Mike bid Omi a goodnight, and each of them returned to their homes for the night.

‡ot ‡ater

The wind blew, rattling the window in Mike and Gus's room. The panes faced north, and they were not insulated well. Frost built up around the edges, a draft developed, and Mike slowly lifted his eyelids. He struggled to see through his morning blur, but the draft told him the truth. It was snowing, and the wind was blowing the snow around and around just outside his window. "Gus, wake up," he called. "Look at the snow."

Gus rolled over, turning his face from Mike. "I just wanna sleep; leave me alone," he grumbled.

"It's 9:30, Gus. We overslept! You have to get up. You told your dad you would watch the station again. He's got that service call out at Dale's."

Gus threw the heavy square patch quilt off onto the floor. "Oh, man! You're right. I'll bet he's steamin'!"

"I'll go call the station; you get ready. I'll talk to him a little and see if he's mad," Mike said as he bolted out of the room. He didn't run far. His aunt, Cara Lee, was standing in the hall. By the statement she made, she had overheard the boys. Cara Lee was Gus's mother, but she had mothered Mike for a number of years, and he had gotten to know her well. She meant business.

"Yes, you just call and see how mad he is . . . Save your steps, he just called *me*. Gus, get yourself up right now and get to the station. Lucky for you it snowed, and the station is slow. But he's waiting on you," she said in no uncertain terms. Mike stepped aside and managed to leave the room without any consequences for trying to cover for Gus.

Missing breakfast, the boys bundled up in their wool jackets, scarves, mittens, and hats. They hurried up the road to the station and found Clair about to leave for a repair job on a farmer's tractor. "About time, Gus," he called from the window of his truck, sounding a bit upset. "I'll be back soon. It shouldn't take too long."

"I have to check my rabbit trap," Mike said as he walked into the station store.

"Oh, yeah, you set a trap yesterday, didn't you?" Gus said with interest.

"I told Omi I'd check it today. I better get over there."

"Not so fast. You're goin' over to the Iceberg to get me some breakfast," Gus ordered. "Tell Mrs. Wagner to put it on our bill. I'll tell dad he doesn't have to pay me. I'll eat instead."

"Aw, Gus, if you'd get out of bed," Mike said as he left, pushing open the Main Street side door. He walked down the sidewalk until he came to the familiar green and white tiled entrance. The blown wisps of snow had been swept with a broom, so he stomped his feet near the curb and then entered the diner.

It was not full of customers as usual, and he realized he had overslept much later than he normally did on his days off. The diner was hot for a winter day, and he removed his wool jacket. The smell of Christmas baking filled the dining room.

The smell of cake, chocolate, fresh bread, bacon, and biscuits attacked his nose in a barrage of scents that confused his belly. But bacon won out over cake this time, and he smiled at Mrs. Wagner as she caught his eye from the kitchen. "Mikey, come in and have a seat. Are you enjoying the snow? I'll get you your favorite. Have a seat."

"Well, I have to take some breakfast to Gus at the station, so I'll get mine in a bag, too, if you don't mind," he said. "That bacon smells very good. I want that on a biscuit and a little gravy. Gus will take his usual, I guess."

"OH, MY!" Mrs. Wagner screamed as a large pot of water and contents crashed down and spilled across the floor. Water splashed across the room

and onto Mike's jacket he had just laid across a counter stool. Steam rose up and covered the back kitchen. "Mike, gather the towels from the counter, please!" she yelled.

Mike and another customer ran to her aid. They threw the rags over the water covering the floor. "Don't touch the water yet, Mike! It's hot. You'll burn your hands," she called. The other man stepped on the rags as Mike added more. Mrs. Wagner turned off the gas to the stovetop and picked up the boiled cabbage and pot from the floor.

"What were you cooking, Mrs. Wagner?" Mike asked. "It smells funny back here."

"Oh," she said with a laugh. The German folks around here love boiled cabbage, so I cook it around Christmas. The Klein's family reunion is this afternoon down at the fire hall," she said.

Mike joined Mrs. Wagner, who was now down on her knees picking up wet towels. "I turned into the pot and knocked it off. I'm not used to this oversized pot sitting so close to the edge. I usually have it on the back burner. Oh, well, I'll start over, I guess."

Mike picked up the heavily stained rags from the floor and placed them in the sink to drain. Eventually, the floor was dried, and Mrs. Wagner cleaned and sterilized the pot for another go.

"Mike, I'll feed you and Gus for free this morning, but help me one last time. Run up the street to the grocery store and ask Gill for another red cabbage. He'll bill me," she said.

"Sure thing, Mrs. Wagner. I'll be right back."

Mike grabbed his wet jacket and ran out toward the grocery store, but he returned empty-handed. "He's out of red cabbage, Mrs. Wagner. Bern Ebner bought the last one this morning."

"Well, I know he's German, but that man buys more red cabbage than any German I've ever seen. He can't possibly eat that much cabbage. I'll bet he's feedin' those dirty pigs of his," she said with distain. "He butchered one last year and tried selling me some bacon slabs, but I couldn't afford his price. It must be the high price of groceries he's buyin' 'em." She laughed. "He's not a butcher anyway, he's a farmer."

"We saw a whole box leave with him yesterday," Mike said.

Mrs. Wagner handed him two bags of breakfast. He thanked her and left for the station as soon as he could. If the cold air cooled the food too much, Gus would complain, so he ran up the street and entered the station. He was surprised to see Omi's mother standing at the counter, talking with Gus. She seemed upset, so Mike sat on a bench and quietly listened to their conversation, holding his bagged breakfast.

"Well, Ma'am, Mike is right here. You can ask him yourself, but I'm pretty sure he didn't do it," Gus said with concern.

"Do what?" Mike replied as he stood handing Gus his breakfast.

"Did you take a large male rabbit from our barn last night? Ever since she met you boys, her rabbits have started disappearing. They can't get out of that stall by themselves." She was angrier than Mike had noticed, but he couldn't believe his ears. *Is this what Omi thinks? Does she think I'm taking her rabbits?* His mind was racing, his stomach seemed sick all of a sudden, and his knees felt weak. He stood for a long moment looking at her but finally spoke.

"You think I—, umm, we took Omi's rabbits? Why would we do that?" he answered.

"Where do you think a large white rabbit would disappear to? You're the only people who know she has rabbits in that barn." She turned her face to the window, looking out into the parking lot of the station. "Look at her! She's crying, still."

Mike dropped his breakfast bag on the counter and ran out through the customer entrance door to Omi. He knocked on the window of the truck. It startled her, but she opened the door. Mike didn't say a word. He sat down on the seat of the truck as Omi moved towards the middle on the wide bench. She was streaming tears and seemed inconsolable for a moment, but Mike quieted her as he placed his arm around her in an awkward but caring way. She laid her head on his arm and took deep breaths and eventually stopped crying.

"You know I didn't take your rabbits, right?" he asked.

"Yes, I don't think you did. It's my mother who said that. I'm sorry."

"Oh, good," Mike said. "I didn't want to lose you as a friend. I would never do that."

"It is my fault, I guess. I told her how much you like rabbits, so Officer Satrang is planning to look in your garage today. I am really sorry," she said.

"He can look all he wants. There ain't no rabbits in there," he said.

Mike climbed all the way into the truck and pulled the door shut. He sat up and brought his arm down to face her. "Omi, are you sure your big male is missing; maybe he's under the straw or dug a hole to keep warm. It is cold outside."

"I went into the stall and looked everywhere. He's gone. Somebody took him for sure. There's no way out of that pen. He was stolen. I think there were tracks, too, but the snow-covered everything up. I saw one faint track under the eve of the barn rounding the corner, but everything else is covered. I know he was stolen, but who would do that?" she asked, not expecting a response.

"There's just too many strange things about rabbits around here. My mother wants to move back to the reservation because of it. She wanted some ponies this spring, but now she's scared they'd be stolen, too."

"Oh, no! Please don't leave, Omi. I–" he stopped short of his last words, and Omi looked up at him.

"I know, Mike. I don't want to leave, either. My father once said, 'If you leave what you do not like, you will never change it. That is a bad thing. If you leave what you like, you will also never change it. That is a good thing.' And I think that's true."

"What does that even mean?" Mike asked.

"It means you can change the bad things and leave the good things alone," she explained.

"I'll go talk to your mother. We'll get to the bottom of this if I have to stay the night in that barn," he said firmly. "Plus, we have a trap to check!"

Omi smiled big at him. He opened the truck's door to leave and walked up to the window where her mother stood. He quietly mouthed the words to her, "You can't leave." She motioned for him to come in.

"I do not want to leave, but if Willow City is not honest, we cannot stay. My Chippewa people say *gimoodwin* is bad sign," Omi's mother said.

"I don't know what that means, but I believe you," he said.

"*Gimoodwin* means taking another's possessions, and it is not the way of the Chippewa."

"It's not our way, either. I would never steal from you or anyone else. But you have to give us time to solve this blue rabbit thing. I might be able to get her a blue rabbit. If you stay, she can help me. She'd be the only one with a blue rabbit. That would cheer her up." Mike stood by to see what she would say.

"I am sorry. I should have listened to her. I know you did not take her rabbits. I do not want to leave, so maybe we could use your help."

"Ma'am, did you still want some gas?" Gus asked, breaking up the mood.

"Oh, yes, please. Just put in three dollars," she said.

Mike immediately ran to the truck and began pumping the gas. Gus stepped out with Omi's mother. "That's my job, you know!" he said with a chuckle.

"Well, Omi and I are in a hurry to see the trap we set last night," Mike said excitedly.

Omi nodded her head as she rolled down the window. "I'll bet we caught that blue rabbit. Everybody will believe Gunder *now*."

The wind was still blowing, and the temperature seemed to be getting colder. In the distance, Mike noticed his uncle coming up the road in the truck. He seemed to be in a hurry as he pulled alongside Mike and Omi. Mike was finished pumping the fuel and was putting the cap on the tank.

"Jump in, Mike; I need your help over at Dale's. You'll have to pull the tractor so I can get it started. Gus, stay here until I get back. Let's go!"

"But Clair, I have plans with Omi. We need to check the trap."

"Later! You'll pay me with your time like I told you on Sunday. I need help today, and you're it. Now, let's go."

Omi looked disappointed, but she knew Mike had to listen to the adults in his life. Mike was also crushed; he held his head low as he walked to Clair's truck. "Aww, get in, Mike. I've thawed that tractor out with a blowtorch; she'll freeze up again if we don't get back there. You'll have to drive the truck and pull me to get it runnin'." He seemed anxious as he placed the truck in drive.

Mike hollered out the window to Omi. "I'll pick you up as soon as I get back; just don't leave without me."

Clair and Mike worked on the customer's tractor for hours. Mike was beside himself for most
of the time. He wondered how Omi was feeling.
He wondered if she had taken off on a long walk
out to Gunder's or if she was just sitting at home
watching out the window for him. It was getting
late, but Mike pulled the tractor with the truck
one last time. A large puff of smoke billowed out
of the stack, and a lady and her husband came
running out of the house on the hill. Clair waved
his hands for Mike to stop pulling. The tractor
had snorted back to life.

"Can we go now, Clair?" he asked.

"I guess. Let me finish up here, and we'll leave."

Winter in North Dakota was hard on machines,
but many residents used their tractors in the winter to clear snowy driveways, feed livestock, and
grade the highways. Clair was very important to
Willow City. His mechanic skills kept many of the
cars and tractors running. But Mike couldn't appreciate that at the moment. He pestered Clair
again. "I just have to check the trap we set yesterday, Clair. Omi is waiting, too."

"Alright, Mikey! I'm ready. Let me collect my pay, and we'll be off."

It was only a short ride back to the Cenex station, but to Mike's chagrin, the sun was setting. Wintertime in the north had short days, and at six o'clock, it was nearly dark. The white of the snow reflected the bleak light of the sky, giving a needed reprieve from darkness. Mike jumped out of the car and ran inside. "Gus, can you drive me over to Omi's house? We have to check the trap!" He was in a panic, but Clair walked in behind him.

"Take the boy out to Gunder's, but make it quick. It's getting late. Drive the old truck sitting around back." Clair seemed to finally get the excitement Mike had been feeling. Mike understood it as appreciation.

"Thanks, Clair."

"I don't know why I have to take you. I've worked here all day by myself," Gus said with an irritated tone.

"You may be the first to see a blue rabbit, Gus."

"I doubt it, Mikey. But if you say so, you'll have to prove it."

Mike ran out in front of Gus. Trying to follow, Gus felt a strong hand grip his arm. "Son, look out for that old Bern; I don't trust him. Earlier, Omi's mother told me what happened. Don't argue with the man if he bothers you. It's getting dark, so I guess if Mike just has to check the trap, better now than in daylight. Look after them all, ya' hear?"

Having to watch the station for the day was boring, but his father was seeing him as capable. "Yes, sir. I will," he said stalwartly.

.

CHAPTER EIGHT

A Mysterious Find

The boys jumped in the 1940 Chevy truck parked behind the building. He had driven it around town three weeks ago. He had talked his mother into a ride on a lazy Sunday afternoon. He wondered if it would start, but the old 6-volt starter kicked the engine well, and they were headed west down Main Street despite the cold and the snow.

"STOP!" Mike yelled suddenly. "Deevee and Levi are in the diner; let's get them, too."

Gus slid the truck to a stop. "I'll wait right here. You run in," Gus said as Mike jumped out of the truck. "And hurry!"

The doors of the diner flew open as Deevee and Levi sat at the counter. The winter evenings were slow, and their mother had just finished catering the Klein family reunion at the Fire Hall. The boys had washed up the dishes and were enjoying a game of checkers. "Guys, do you want to ride with us to Gunder's to check the trap we set yesterday?"

Their mother overheard the question as she came out of the back. "Who's driving?"

"My uncle's lettin' Gus drive me out, but I'm sure it's okay if your boys ride along," Mike replied.

"Well, I'd rather they take their tractor out. I'm not sure I want my boys riding with Gus. He's a little young to be driving that truck. I know he knows how to drive, but I don't think Officer Satrang would want four boys out on the East and West in a pickup truck," she said.

Gus and Mike had been seen driving around town before in the old truck, but driving around town at night was different. They drove slowly and carefully and usually just around the station or short errands for Clair, and it was always during the day. She had nothing against Gus, but speeds out on the gravel roads were as fast as the highway speeds at times, and Mrs. Wagner knew that a fresh snowfall could make the roads treacherous, not to mention it was getting late.

"You boys can go, but take your tractor. You need to get it home anyway," she said.

An old worn truck horn sounded as Deevee and Levi donned their coats, hats, and scarves. Mike rattled the bells on the diner door as he sailed out, jumped in the truck, and slapped Gus on the knee. "They'll meet us out there; let's get Omi."

Gus continued west for a short distance and turned north for Omi's house. She was doing exactly as Mike had pondered, looking out the window into the dimming street waiting for signs of a visitor.

He saw her jump to attention as the lights of the old truck pulled into the drive. Her mother's truck was not there. A sick feeling welled up in Mike's stomach. He assumed Omi's mother would not let her go with two boys near dark in hunt of a blue rabbit. But Mike had to stop and ask; he had promised he would. As late as it was, snowy North Dakota nights were not that dark. The light from the moon, and even the stars, was reflected off the snow-covered landscape; every night was a winter wonderland. There would be plenty of light to see the trap. He felt better as Omi ran out of the house and jumped into the truck. They had waited for a short while as she gathered her winter coat, boots, and mittens.

"Your mother, did you ask your mother? I should go speak with her," Mike said, but suspected she was gone.

"She is not here, and I told her I would be with you. She knows we were going to check the trap. If I am not here when she gets home, she will know I am with you. It will not take long to see. Then we will come right back. I am sure we will beat her home, anyway."

"Where did she go?" Gus asked.

"Oh, she's over at the fire hall with a friend. I told her we would be near Gunder's place if we went; she is fine. Let's go!"

Gus looked at Mike for reassurance and placed the truck in reverse. Mike nodded his head. He loved the way Omi talked in completed sentences, so sure and direct, and it made him feel better.

They continued a mile west out of town and turned north for the East and West. Soon, the large, blue-green spruce trees could be seen in the distance against the winter white of the prairie. Further still, a single headlight on the cub tractor was coming over a gentle rise in the road. Deevee and Levi had wasted no time in leaving the diner, and they were nearly there as they had taken the road north from the Cenex station to connect to the East and West.

At the prompting of Mike, Gus stopped the truck along the side of the road and let the two of them out near the trap. Gus pulled into Gunder's drive just behind Deevee and Levi. He pulled in front of them and waved his arms for them to follow. The truck and tractor pulled through the snow into the grove of spruce trees next to the drive. Deevee and Levi looked cold but were bundled in their hats and wool scarves wrapped about their necks twice over. Eventually, they greeted each other. "Why are we pulled into the trees, Gus?" they asked.

"Okay, listen. Omi's mother told my dad about Bern dumping you over the fence. My dad told me to bring Mike out and to watch out for old man Bern. I think he's a little nervous about us being out here. I'm just making sure Bern won't know we're out here if he comes by. Mike and Omi are on his property again."

Unexpectedly, a light came on at Gunder's house. The door creaked open, and Gunder stood in his housecoat and night cap.

"Who be dere?" he called.

Deevee and Levi ran the distance to the house. Their faces turned redder, but this time from the warm blood finally coursing through their veins after a cold ride out. They yelled toward Gunder as they ran in his direction. "It's Deevee and Levi, and Mike and Omi. Just checking the trap we set yesterday. Is that okay?"

"Vell, I see—late ya' know. I vondered vhat dat noise is, you see."

"We won't be long, Gunder. We'll be right back after we check the trap," Deevee said. "Sorry to bother you, sir."

"Vell, you get dose blue hares!" he said as he closed the door and turned off the light.

Mike and Omi were nearing the trap. They cautiously walked toward it, but Omi stopped Mike with her right hand. "Look!" she said. "Look here in the snow. What is that?"

Mike studied it carefully, but he couldn't determine what it was with the limited light. Something had stained the top surface of the snow. "Gus, see if there's a light in the truck," he yelled.

"Not so loud, Mike, and I have a light in my pocket," Omi said.

"Sorry, you're right. I think Gunder turned on his yard light for a moment."

Omi shined the light on the stained snow. They looked at each other with surprise; the two stood nearly frozen and unable to speak. Slowly, they looked down again in astonishment. Carefully, Mike bent down and touched the stain, scooping some snow in his un-mittened hand. Amid the numerous rabbit tracks, the snow was stained blue, a beautiful sky blue. It was all about in small patches but leading towards the trap.

"How can this be?" Omi asked. "I do not understand."

But, before Mike could answer, they all heard it, Gus, Deevee, Levi, Mike, and Omi—the snorting of an old Oliver tractor coming up the road from the east. Across the road, Mike could scarcely make out the other three running for the spruce trees to hide. They knew it was Bern, too. Omi and Mike dove into the snow behind the brush. They could not be seen on Bern's property, and Omi quickly turned out the light and stuffed it in her pocket.

The tractor made its way toward them. All seemed quiet, and everybody was out of sight. It was as dark as it would get for a winter night on the plains; even a partial lit moon would make the white landscape glow. Still, Bern shined his bright spotlight up and down the road. He covered both sides of the ditches as if looking for something. He shined the light over Omi and Mike's head several times, into the spruce trees, and then back into the ditches. Mike could smell the fuel from the tractor's engine as it traveled by. It made him uneasy to think Bern was so close. He prayed he would not spot the wooden trap. He wondered if Bern had seen them or if this was something he did on occasion.

Mike's fingers were cold as he had taken off his mitten to look at the blue stains. Omi was starting to shiver, having to lie in the snow. Fortunately, the tractor turned around farther down the road and hurried past them from the direction it had come. Once clear, the boys and Omi came out of hiding and waved at each other from across the way. As the tractor cleared the gentle rise in the road, Omi turned on her flashlight. Mike was still looking across the road, and Omi caught sight of the back of his coat.

"Oh, Mike, I meant to ask you about that stain on the back of your jacket. I saw it earlier, just didn't think about it. Come here; I think it's the same color as the snow stains."

The two compared the color and looked perplexed. "It's from the pot at the diner. Mrs. Wagner spilled a kettle of boiling water, it splashed everywhere, including on my coat. I thought it was just wet. Come to think of it, those new white rags she bought were all stained, too. I think it was the same color."

The wooden box trap had been sprung. The stick was not holding the edge of the box as they left it. It didn't mean something was in it, only that something had pulled on the carrot. Mike watched Omi as she walked to the trap, squatted down, and placed her hand under the box. "Stop, Omi!" he yelled in a protective tone. "We don't know what's under there! That could be a fox, or badger, or something that could bite!"

"Okay, come and hold the light for me." Omi laid her face in the snow as low as she could. Mike shined the light under the edge of the box. "I see it! I see it! Lift it a little more, Mike!" She shoved her hand under and took hold of the hind leg of a rabbit. "Lift the box, Mike!" she hollered.

A blue rabbit began kicking and squealing for freedom. Omi covered it with both hands and took a firm grip. She brought it to her chest and cuddled it carefully but steadily. Mike was speechless, but only for a time.

"Guys!" he finally yelled. "Come over here right away. We got one! We got a blue rabbit!"

"*Nanabozho!*" Omi yelled. Mike could hear the emotion in her voice. She began to cry, and she buried her head in his fir behind his ears.

"What does that mean?" Mike asked.

"It's Nanabozho! My male!"

"That's your rabbit?"

"Yes, look at his ear. He has a piece missing from his left ear. It's him. It's Nanabozho! Somebody stained him blue. Look at his tail; poor thing, it's all matted."

"Omi, the blue is coming off on your coat—and your face, too." Mike laughed as he wiped her tears with his mitten.

The others came trudging through the ditch and up to the trap site. They all stood amazed at the blue rabbit. Mike was holding the flashlight on it as they all noticed the white fur on its bottom side. "I think the dye didn't take too well; it's coming off on everything," Gus said.

Omi felt sorry for her rabbit. "Aww, the hair on his back is all matted, too. This is something I have never seen before. Why is my rabbit blue?" Omi looked at the boys, then at Mike. The look on her face expressed distrust with them all. After a long pause, she came out with it. "Is this some kind of joke you are playing on me, Mike?"

"Omi. No! I didn't know about any of this. But we can all see the rabbit is blue. There's a trick being played, but on who I don't know." He bent down and put his hand on her back. "Omi, I'm your friend, and I would not dishonor that. I feel very happy I've gotten to know you. I'm gonna help figure this out, okay? Please don't think that any of us did this. I was very excited about finding a blue rabbit, too. Please, Omi."

"It must be Gunder. He's the crazy one with the blue rabbit stories. He scares me," Gus said.

"Yeah, he wants it to be true, so he can claim all that stuff he talks about," Deevee added.

Levi questioned them all. "But he wants rid of the blue rabbits; it doesn't make sense that he would create them to torment himself, does it?"

Omi snuggled her rabbit. "I hope it's *anybody* but you guys. Mike's been crazy about finding a blue rabbit, ya' can't hide that fact. And Gus has been too busy at the station to have done it. Same with Deevee and Levi always washing dishes. I'm sorry, forget what I said. I just want to take my rabbit home and give him a bath. He did not deserve any of this, poor thing! He is shivering, too. I hope Gunder does not see him; he will shoot him!"

"Whoa, Omi, Gunder has to see him. I won't get my pop gun, I mean my new BB gun, if we don't show it to him," Mike quipped.

"Yeah, we have to see his reaction to the blue rabbit. It might tell us if he's telling the truth. We'll all watch his reaction; we have to," Levi explained.

"But he will want to take him from me. Look what he did yesterday. Your father kept him from shooting all of us."

"Omi," Mike interrupted, "we'll show him it's blue dye; it's not a real blue rabbit. I don't think he's doin' it. He won't do nothin' to a white rabbit."

Levi and Gus were shaking their heads, then Gus spoke. "It's Gunder. He put on a good show, all to make it believable."

"Now that I think about it, that's what I think, too," Levi said with his arm folded.

"Come on, guys, let's go see him and put this to rest," Mike ordered.

Omi was hesitant but got up and followed the boys down the ditch and across the road to Gunder's house. It was a long walk up the drive, and Omi felt scared of the old man whom she didn't really know. She told the boys that she would not let go of her Nanabozho. She also wanted to know where her other two rabbits were.

Not What it Seems

Gus knocked on the door several times. The porch light came on as the door screaked open. Hot air came out as he pushed the door open. Gunder had apparently been sleeping by the fireplace in his reading chair when he was startled awake by the knock. He tried to make sense of the four boys and a girl holding a blue rabbit, all standing on his porch. Suddenly, he yelled out, "Get dat blue hare away from my house. You take it far away from here. Vhy you bring it here? You will jinx my house!"

Omi turned and jumped off the porch running in the deep snow.

"Omi, Omi, come back!" the boys yelled. She stopped, but kept her back to Gunder embracing her rabbit tightly.

"Gunder, listen to me! It's not real, Gunder! Somebody painted it blue with dye. It's really a white rabbit." Mike was desperate for him to hear. "Do you understand, Gunder?"

Gunder stood perplexed. "Not real blue hare? Vhy? Who vould do dat? I see other blue hares before now, right here in my farmyart. They are bat luck for me."

"Well, this one is not a real blue rabbit; can we show you?" Mike asked.

"Vi vil, I sure don't like the hare, but I see it. Bring it closer," he said.

"You have to promise not to hurt it first," Omi called.

"Ya, ya, let me see white hare."

Deevee and Levi helped Omi back up onto the porch. "I don't think he's behind any of it now," Deevee whispered to her.

"He better not hurt my Nanabozho."

Gunder would not touch the blue rabbit, but he acknowledged the blue dye and the white rabbit under it. "I have seen da blue stains on my barn door, on my outhouse. Dat I know."

Levi tried his approach. "We think all the blue rabbits are dyed blue, Gunder. We're just not sure who's doing it. Um—um, you wouldn't be doin' that, would you? Um, I mean, as a joke to go along with your stories?"

Gunder turned to his right and stepped aside. The others looked at Levi in a nervous gaze. Quickly, he returned with a picture of his sister. "Dis is my beautiful sister, Vigdis. Dose blue hares took my sveet Vigdis. I loved her very much. I vould not have anyting to do vith blue hares, boy!"

"I'm sorry, Gunder," Mike quickly covered. "He didn't mean anything by it. But we've solved the blue rabbit story, right?"

"Mike, you be paintin' da hares blue. Vhy vould I do it? You want my pop gun. You try to fool ol' Gunder?"

Mike stood with his mouth open, Omi's eyes widened in understanding, Deevee and Levi looked at each other in ponder, but Gus had his back. "Gunder, you know that Mike has been trying to help you all this time. Tell us who you really think's doin' it."

"I don't know vhy somebody vould do dat. Come spring, I vill be movin' into town. I von't vorry about it anymore. I yust hope it's not you boys. You tell me who it be that paints the hares blue, and I give you my pop gun. I tink dat is fair. Den we see vhy." He shut the door rather hard, and it gave the impression he was not happy. Omi shook her head as she looked at Mike.

"What?" Mike questioned in an unbelieving tone.

"I want to go home now," she said.

They all walked slowly to the truck and tractor parked in the trees. Deevee and Levi asked Gus to follow the tractor with his truck, but only as far as the turn north towards their ranch. The tractor had only one working head light, and the extra light from the truck was much safer on the road at night. Eventually, they came to the turn which led to Deevee and Levi's ranch, but the road also ran between Bern Ebner's properties. He owned fields on both sides of the road. Gus and Mike noticed Bern's tractor parked near an old granary in the field on the right. Old boxes were piled up near the door of the shed, and a faint light was glowing through the top gable hatch.

"That's Bern's tractor. I wonder if he's in there," Mike said.

Gus slowed the truck as Deevee turned left with a wave of his hand. The night air was getting cold again, and the white steamy clouds of exhaust vapor poured from the little red Cub tractor. He continued north out of sight as Gus rolled slowly on. Fortunately, Deevee and Levi's mother came up the road. She slowed to a stop, rolled her window down, and asked the boys if there was trouble.

"Oh, no, Ma'am," Gus spoke as he opened the truck door; the window handle was missing. "We were just following your boys home. One of their lights is out. They're just in front of you; you can catch 'em in short order."

"Well, thank you, Gus. How did the rabbit hunting go? Did you bag one?" Mrs. Wagner asked.

Mike yelled across Gus and Omi, "We found the blue rabbit, Mrs. Wagner, but it's not what you think. Omi held up the rabbit, but with no light on in the truck, it was not as spectacular as Mike had wished.

"Oh, my!" she said. "A real blue rabbit?"

"It's just dyed blue, Mrs. Wagner. Your boys will tell you all about it," Gus explained.

"Sounds like a good trick," she said, laughing.

"Yes, Ma'am," Gus said politely. He said his goodbyes, and they continued on their ways.

Omi stayed quiet but held her blue rabbit tighter as it slept in her arms. Mike stared out the window as the truck rolled down the moonlit road. The word

"trick" stayed in his mind as he considered the pos-
sibility that somebody was out to make a fool of him.
He knew what Omi was thinking but said nothing.
He pictured Omi's rabbit nestled in the dried grass
and wondered if the rabbit was in on it, too.

Eventually, they made their way to Omi's house, and
Omi's mother looked upset as she stepped out. Her
expression quickly changed as she saw the blue rabbit under the porch light. Gus and Levi could only
imagine the story Omi was telling her mother about
the evening's events. Her mother's hand, too, became
blue as she held the whitening rabbit.

Pondering the blue rabbit origins, all five slept
well. Mike's late morning calls arranged for a
meeting in the nest at six o'clock p.m. It was later
than Omi wanted, but the boys had responsibili-
ties, even during their Christmas vacation. But
this time they would vote on allowing a girl into
the nest. Gus and Mike arrived first, and Deevee
and Levi rode into town with their father since he
had business in town. Across the road, Omi waited on the bench under the streetlamp bundled in
her winter layers.

"Aww, come on, Omi. You know we're gonna let you in," Gus said.

"Are you goin' soft, Gus? You're the one who said no girls," Levi reminded.

"I'm trading you out for her."

"Very funny. Let's get up there," Levi responded.

They climbed through the window of the old filling station and up the slatted wall ladder into the attic. Mike chivalrously went up behind Omi. He reassured her he'd catch her if she fell. Levi rolled his eyes at Deevee. "He'll probably trip her so she'll fall into his arms, ooh!" Levi teased.

Gus took his seat in the old rocking chair, but he felt a little larger due to the winter gear he was wearing. He lit several candles for light. Omi didn't seem too impressed as she walked around the boxes and things strewn in the attic. She was also watching where she stepped as not to fall through the ceiling at Mike's warning.

"You better stay down below, Mike." Deevee decided to join in the teasing. "You can catch her if she falls through."

Omi stood up for herself. "I ain't nobody's girl. I'm just one of you, for now. Let's get this meeting started." She sat down on an old metal bucket and faced Gus. The faint light in the attic gave them all a sense of equality, and even though Gus sat on the rocker, Omi started the meeting. She was not clear on the meeting rituals and rules of order, but the boys didn't protest. The meeting was about her rabbits anyway.

"I'm sure you all went to bed thinking about this blue rabbit thing. I want you to know that I have thought a lot about it, too. I am sure, now, that Mike didn't take my rabbits. He seems honest to me, and my mother said if I had questions, I should not accuse without proof." Mike smiled at her. "My first question is, when did Gunder start seeing the blue rabbits?"

"Oh, I know that one, Omi," Mike said quickly. "He told me he saw one in the fall and two this past week."

"If my rabbits were stolen this week, then whose rabbits did he see, and were they really blue?"

"That's a good question, but who's doin' it?" Gus asked. "It's not us."

Mike stood up. "Deevee, your mom spilled hot water on my jacket, and it turned it blue. Was she making some kind of paint? I remember the rags were all stained, and it was a blue color, the same color as the rabbit. I also heard her laugh at me last night in the truck. Do you think she's pullin' some kind of trick on me? That's what she said. I've thought hard on this."

"It has to be somebody we know since that is what we have all been talking about," Omi said.

"It's not *our* mother!" Levi said. "I can tell you that."

"How did it all get started then?" Omi questioned.

"Omi, I was chasing jackrabbits in the fields on Saturday when I ran into Gunder on the East and West. That's when he told *me* about it. That's the truth. You've heard the rest, at least, what we know about old Gunder. He is crazy, but he's seein' blue rabbits. We have the proof, a blue rabbit!"

A strange hush filled the nest. Mike placed his hands on his head as if holding down his hat, then, suddenly, Mike slapped his knee. "Wait! I got it—Deevee, can you get your mother to speak with us again, like we did when we found that limb along the railroad tracks? I need her to take us on a little drive tonight."

"Um, I guess I can ask her. What are you thinking now? Where do you want to meet her?"

"In the diner. The back corner booth, but tonight after she closes," Mike said.

"She's probably closing now; it's after six and very slow."

Omi and the other boys looked at each other. "What are you planning?" Omi asked. "I want to talk about this some more."

"No time! Let's go. I've got this thing solved, come on," Mike said as he nearly jumped down out of the attic. "Deevee! Let Deevee out next. He's got to get to his mother."

Mike nearly pushed Deevee out of the back-alley window, "Tell her we'll be right there."

Deevee ran across Main Street, his breath hot and humid; it left a trail of vapor in the cold night air. The diner door was still unlocked. The other boys and Omi could see him through the window trying to seat her in the back corner booth. "Mom, do you remember the night we found those two thieves in the south fields?" She nodded her head. "You told me it was a lot of fun, and it reminded you of high school. Remember?" She nodded again. "Let's do it again tonight; we need a little help.

"Oh, no, Deevee. We gave your father a heart attack that night. He didn't know where we went."

"I'll call him and tell him we'll be a little late; it's okay."

The others walked through the door and ended up shoulder to shoulder as if on marching orders.

"Did you ask her, Deevee?"

"I'm trying, Mike."

"Mrs. Wagner, I just need your help to take us out near Gunder's place," Mike said.

"Near Gunder's place?" she asked.

"Yes, right where the turn is to your road. It's just too cold to walk, and too late," Mike clarified.

"Then we can come back here?" she asked.

"Yes, Ma'am, I really need to show everybody something, but I don't want to ruin the surprise. If I'm right, we can call Officer Satrang again."

"Let me lock up first."

Omi and the boys let out a cheer. "Hey, what are we cheering about? I want to talk about this some more," Omi said again.

The clock was ticking ever so late, so it was important for Deevee to let his father know they would be home later. In no time, the middle schoolers were piled into the yellow Ford Fairlane with Omi, Mike, and Gus in the back and the Wagners in the front. Mike leaned over the front seat and pointed the way like George Washington crossing the Delaware River.

"I think I know the way to the road home," she said as the others laughed and pushed and pulled him into the back seat.

CHAPTER TEN

SNOOPS

In minutes, they arrived at the turn. "Stop here but pull into that approach, and turn your lights off," Mike ordered, Mrs. Wagner turned and looked at him.

"Mike, what are you going to do?" Mrs. Wagner asked.

"Okay, it's time you hear this; now don't interrupt, or I'll have to start over." The windows in the car were starting to fog up as Mike began rambling question after question. "Do you remember Gill giving Bern a box of red cabbage? Mrs. Wagner, could you get another red cabbage to cook yesterday? Guys, do you remember somebody with dirty stained hands? Mrs. Wagner, what happened to the rags when we wiped up the hot water? And what is this stain on my jacket?"

"Oh, I see," Mrs. Wagner said.

"See what?" Omi asked, followed by the others.

"When you boil red cabbage, the water turns blue. It's a dye color used for many years," she said.

With sternness in his voice, Mike said, "Look at Bern's granary in the field. See those boxes by the door? Those are from the grocery store, and they're produce boxes. The kind that red cabbage comes in! Can you see the light in the hatch door? Somebody is working with red cabbage. Come on!"

Mike pushed Omi to open the door, and he crawled over her. He began walking toward the granary building. Gus called for him to come back, but he kept walking. Mrs. Wagner called as well. "Oh, this is trespassing for sure. I sure don't want to see Bern tonight. MIKE, get back here before I tell your uncle!" she hollered. "What if he's in there?"

Mike called back. "There's no truck or tractor here. Please! I've got to see in there." His breath was hot and warm, and he was breathing heavy as he tripped over the ruts in the snow made by a tractor earlier in the day. His mind was made up, and it was reminiscent of Gus's refusal to turn back the night he met the Hairy Farmer's Daughter. Gus's attitude had rubbed completely off onto Mike, but even Gus was unsure about going into one of Bern's buildings. The timid Mike of the past had given way to the new and improved Mike. If there was going to be a hero in this adventure, Mike was determined to be one for Omi.

Levi, again, described it all too well. "You're just showing off for Omi. You're gonna get us all in trouble."

For years, the old wooden granary was used for storing grains after harvest. However, sturdier buildings were erected with much larger capacity. Many farmers turned the field granaries into equipment sheds, or small livestock barns, or feed storage. On this building, a usable walk-in door had been added, and there was a faint light coming from the gable end hatch door once used to auger in grain. It was obvious to Mike, and even the others, that this building was being used for other purposes.

"Oh, that boy! Wait 'til I get my hands on him," Mrs. Wagner said as she marched out after him.

The rest of the group followed. They slammed their car doors loudly. It made Mrs. Wagner nervous enough to turn around and look.

"Do you all have to follow?" she asked as she rolled her eyes.

Mike cracked open the door, unsure what he would find, then threw it open without concern. He stood motionless as if something frightened him. He turned his eyes toward them all. The faint light coming from the open door was enough for the rest to see his expression. A large smile slowly stretched across his face, then he erupted with a common phrase. "I TOLD YOU! Look at this; I knew it!"

The others came quickly to the door. Mrs. Wagner kept them all from going in. The shed had a wooden floor with a concrete block cooking pit in the center. Sitting behind the shed, tanks of heating oil were hooked to lines which ran into it. Large burners were glowing yellow as a big pot of water and red cabbage simmered above. The smell was strong, and the heat poured out through the door. Several cages were in the corner, and a larger galvanized tub sat on wooden legs alongside an old table. Brushes stained blue and dripping hung on nails. Bern was making blue dye from red cabbage on a very large scale. Other pots hanging on the walls indicated they had also been filled with blue coloring. A pile of red cabbage chopped up into small pieces covered a table in the far corner.

Mike ran under Mrs. Wagner's arm. "I just need proof; I'll be right back," he said quickly.

"Mike, stop!" she said.

Disobeying an adult was not like him, but Mrs. Wagner finally got what she had asked for. Mike stopped, but not because of what she said. He was staring off into the right corner of the building. "Omi—you better come here, look," he said softly.

Omi moved closer to the door and stuck her head in to see. Two metal rabbit traps hung from the ceiling by a chain, but just under them sat a white rabbit in a small cage, its left ear sticking above the enclosure. She ran past Mike to release it from the cage. "Oh, my little rabbit, it's okay now," she cried as she opened the cage. She said nothing else and ran out with the rabbit toward the car.

"How do you know that's your rabbit, Omi?" Mrs. Wagner called.

"This is a lop-eared rabbit. It was one that was stolen from me. He took it!" she called back.

Mike continued on his mission. He took off his left mitten and dipped it into the water with the red cabbage. It came out as blue as Omi's male rabbit.

"Why is he chopping up the cabbage?" Gus asked.

Mrs. Wagner explained. "The more you chop it up, the easier it is to get out the dye when you boil it. I think he's trying to concentrate it into a thicker liquid. What a mess. I don't see how he can make that dye stay on a rabbit very long. It'll wash off without the right chemicals."

"We know, Mrs. Wagner. Omi's coat had blue dye on it last night from holding her rabbit," Levi said.

"And the stained rabbit was turning white on its bottom side from the snow," Deevee added.

"We better get Officer Satrang over here since we found one of Omi's rabbits. Bern's a rabbit thief," proclaimed Mike as he walked out of the shed with his blue mitten.

Mrs. Wagner was ready to leave. She looked over both of her shoulders and gathered the group like a mother hen as she scolded Mike for running off like he did. "You need to start listening, boy. You really could've gotten us in trouble."

"Mrs. Wagner, please don't tell Clair I did that tonight. I had to prove to everyone that I wasn't taking Omi's rabbits. Even Officer Satrang thinks I did. I just wanted Omi to know I can be trusted, and all of you, too."

"I believe you, now," Omi said with a smile.

"Now? You said you believed me back in the nest," Mike replied.

"I said I couldn't accuse without proof, so I had to believe you."

Mike playfully pushed her as the rest of the boys laughed. Mrs. Wagner reassured Mike she would handle his discipline sometime in the future. "Now, let's get Officer Satrang out here before Bern finds out what's going on. We need to know why he's doing this to Gunder," she said.

Levi asked an important question, "Is he doing this to Gunder, or is Gunder just messin' things up for Bern? Maybe Bern is doing an experiment."

"We're headed to the ranch to get my husband. We'll share it with him, and he can get Officer Satrang for us. This will be something he should handle. I don't think Bern is going to be too nice when he finds out what we did," Mrs. Wagner said.

"What we did? What *we* did? He's a rabbit thief, and he's cruel to animals. I'll bet he was dipping my rabbits in that dye. Probably holding 'em by the ears. That hurts a rabbit. You can't hold 'em by the ears. Oh, that mean old man," Omi complained. "And I want my other rabbit he took."

"I saw paint brushes, so he was probably brushing it on them," Mike consoled.

When they arrived at the ranch, Deevee and Levi ran in ahead of the others. Their father was eating a peaceful meal as he listened to his favorite radio show. "Whoa, boys, what's the rush?" They began telling their father the good and bad news as the others came in. Mike let them speak, as did Mrs. Wagner, but eventually, their father had heard enough. He stood up in an angry manner and pushed in his chair. "I know why Bern is doing that. It's always about the same thing with that man. I don't know how many times he's bothered me, but I'm not selling my land to him. He's trying to run Gunder out of here to get his land, and he'll cut down every last Christmas tree if he does. Bern sent a realtor over to the diner to speak with me. That's one thing, but to scare an old man with blue rabbits, why, that's just wrong!"

"Dad, Gunder said he was moving into town," Levi said.

"No!" Mr. Wagner said. "I hope this thing didn't work. I better get over to Gunder's place and talk to him. I'll get up early and drive over there. But, right now, I'm goin' into town to talk to Officer Satrang."

"Can we go, Dad?" Deevee asked.

"You can all go, but I'm dropping Gus, Mike, and Omi off at their homes. Load up," he said in no uncertain terms.

"Really, Mr. Wagner?" Gus asked with unbelief in his voice.

"I don't mind, Mr. Wagner; I want to go home. I do not want to see Bern anyway. I will visit him in jail," Omi said.

"Okay, sweetheart, I'll get you home first. Looks like you've had a lucky day. That sure is a cute rabbit."

"She is, and I got her back, thanks to Mike. He is a great friend, and she is my favorite rabbit." Omi flipped her rabbit's right ear up and down in a playful manner.

Omi continued talking as the group walked out to the car. "Mike is a hero in a lot of ways. He helped find two of my missing rabbits. I think he needs a reward."

"Oh, he'll get his reward, alright, maybe in the seat of his pants," Mrs. Wagner said in a serious tone. The others laughed as they called his name. "Mikey the rabbit rescuer, Mikey the rabbit rescuer."

The car was crammed, but the old Ford Fairlane was wide enough to handle it. Mr. Wagner put his arm around his wife and turned toward the kids as he put the car in drive. "Say, did you get a chance to see the beautiful glade in the middle of his trees? It's so pretty in the summertime."

Omi and the boys glanced at each other and laughed as they all remembered the encounter with Gunder.

.

CHAPTER ELEVEN

SETTING THINGS RIGHT

Omi was dropped off at home; her mother met them in the driveway. She was very excited to see another one of Omi's rabbits returned to her. "Ominotago, you found another one. I am so happy." She helped Omi out of the car and spoke with Mrs. Wagner for a moment.

"Mike's the hero this time. I think he solved the rabbit thievin' for a while. I'm sure Omi will tell you all about it. Officer Satrang and I will deal with Bern, so I hope you all stay around Willow City for a while. Omi's a great kid. She fits right in with this bunch."

Omi's mother thanked Mr. and Mrs. Wagner for bringing her home and said that she had planned to stay in Willow. Mike was especially happy to hear that, and the boys were poking fun at him. He said nothing back to them but sat with a smile on his face.

Mr. Wagner stopped at the end of the road. He turned sideways to address everyone in the car. "Okay, boys, listen to me closely. Guess what I grabbed on the way out the door? My radio. Officer Satrang gave it to me the night we ran down those two yahoos this past summer. Clair has one, too. I'm sure it's not on, but I'm going to pick him up right now. I want him with us when we confront Bern with all of this blue rabbit stuff."

"Thanks, Mr. Wagner, you're great!" Mike said. "My uncle likes Gunder, so he'll definitely go with us."

"Deevee, call the officer on the radio and ask him if he'll meet us at the station," Mr. Wagner ordered. "Use 10-78 when you get him."

"Yes, sir!" Deevee replied. "I love this radio." He turned the knobs on the radio and pushed the talk button. "Come in, Officer Satrang, come in. Anyone read me?" The static on the radio was soft, then suddenly a reply was heard.

"This is Willow Station; what can I help you with?"

"We have a 10-78. Can you meet us at the Cenex station? This is Deevee Wagner."

"Be right there," the voice returned.

Clair was reading a magazine when they arrived at the station. Mike grabbed him anxiously and dragged him to the car to talk to Mr. Wagner. Clair was all too willing to go. He ran in, turned out the building lights, locked up the till, and locked the doors. He jumped into the front seat with the other adults. Officer Satrang arrived and parked under the streetlight. Mike stepped up to his car window and was allowed to share the entire story with him. As Mike spoke, Clair ran into the station for a short moment.

"I can't imagine a better story," the officer said. "This one will have to go in my book of memoirs. I was headed to your house to look for rabbits the other day, but I got sidetracked. I guess we can forget about that. Sounds like old Bern's stealing, being cruel to animals, and harassing an old man. Anything else you want to throw at him?" He laughed. Mike took a step back. "Oh, I'm not laughing at you, son, just the story. I can't believe a man would go through so much for a piece of land, especially when he has more than he can handle now."

Mr. Wagner pulled the Fairlane near the patrol car. He clarified that bringing the boys would be alright. "I'll need them for witnesses at some point. It might as well be tonight since their parents are here, too. We better get out there before it's too late," the officer said.

He motioned for Mike to get into the patrol car with him. He sat in the front seat. Knowing that Clair had run in for his radio, he asked the officer if he could make a call on his. "Sure, son, just keep in mind that police officers in other small towns could hear you, so make it professional."

"I watch T.V. detective shows; I know some of the calls," he bragged. He took hold of the hand piece and called, "10-98, 10-98, Uncle Clair."

"Whoa, boy I think you better 10-22 that!" the officer said quickly. "You just told him there was a prison break."

"Oops, sorry, 10-22, 10-22!" he called. He quickly corrected his number. "10-49, 10-49, Uncle Clair."

Officer Satrang looked at him with a funny expression. "When have you ever seen a traffic light in Willow City? We don't have a light out. Call 10-22 again, and what are you wanting to say?"

"I want to tell them to follow us," Mike said.

"Oh, I see. Here, I'll show you." Officer Satrang grabbed the hand mic. "Clair, can you follow us, please," he said. He hung the mic on the hook. They both laughed as they headed out of town. Mr. Wagner and the boys in the other vehicle were laughing hysterically.

They drove past the small granary building where the blue dye was being made; Mike pointed it out. All seemed quiet there, so the officer drove on. "We'll be back here in a bit. We'll get Bern to give us a tour of that facility," Officer Satrang said in a sarcastic tone. "I hope you're right about all of this."

The group reached Bern's farm and pulled into the farmyard and up the drive. Pieces of farm equipment, old trucks, and piles of snow-covered manure were everywhere. The barn doors were left open as well as most of the other sheds. It was the exact opposite of Gunder's neat homestead. Officer

Satrang motioned for the group to walk behind him as he knocked on the door. A large dog followed him up the steps and sniffed his knee.

His wife answered the door, "Guten Abend," she said as she addressed them in German.

"Good evening to you, too, Ma'am. I was wondering if I might have a word with your husband. Is Bern home this evening?" he asked.

"No, I mean ya, he is not in zee houze. He is shutding zee gate in zee back pasture. Can I help you?"

"I'm sorry, Ma'am, it is Bern I need. He has some explaining to do."

"Come in, come in you all. You can vait on him here. Pleaze."

The woman seemed overly kind, even pushy. She laid another log on the fire as the others filed in and sat down on a long bench that separated the kitchen from the living room. The boys were shoulder to shoulder, and the four adults stood by the door. It was a lot of people for a small farmhouse. The boys looked extremely nervous about what was going to happen when Bern entered his home.

Mrs. Ebner walked to the front window and looked out. She muttered something about cake, pulled the curtains, and left for the kitchen. The curtains were not of a heavy material, and it wasn't long before Mrs. Wagner saw lights rounding the corner of the front drive. They were heading away from the farm.

"Isn't that Bern's truck?" she yelled. "I think he's leavin!"

Mrs. Ebner returned and stood in front of the door. "You must schtay for cake. He'll be right back, I'm sure."

Officer Satrang kindly moved her out of the way. "Thank you, Ma'am, but we really must be leavin' now. Let's go, everyone!"

Mike jumped in the patrol car before Officer Satrang could get off the steps. The others piled into the Fairlane. A red light came on atop the patrol car, and Officer Satrang led the way as they all sped out of the driveway after Bern. Both cars fishtailed on the road's slippery winter road pack. The boys in the Fairlane were hanging over the front seat of the car, watching for Bern, but the patrol car blocked their view. "Woo hoo!" Mrs. Wagner yelled. "This reminds me of summer."

"I guess we'll see that shed now. I'll bet he's going to destroy the evidence. He must've noticed you were in there today. Otherwise, he wouldn't have expected us," Officer Satrang said.

When they all arrived, Bern had just entered the old granary and was throwing things in the back of his truck. Officer Satrang stepped out of his car. "Bern! Stop right there and come here!" he ordered.

"You schtay out my building, ya' hear!" Bern yelled.

"Come here, Bern!" the officer yelled again. "Mike, tell Clair to come around the other side."

Mike grabbed the radio and relayed the message.

"You schtay off my property, Clair. Und get zoze nozey kids off, too!" Bern continued yelling.

"Come here, Bern. Come here, now, before I get angry with you!" The officer's voice was very demanding. Bern sensed it, too.

"Vy are you here? Zis be my property!" The air was cold, and Bern's breath hung over him like a cloud. The lights of the cars lit up the frosty snow-covered things like a million diamonds. "Vhat did I do? Zere is nozing here for you." He looked around for someone to take his side. His arms were out with his dirty stained palms up, gesturing innocence. It was clear why they were stained. It reminded Mike of a child who denies they stole the chocolate despite the brown smudges around their lips.

"Bern, you have to come here and turn around. I'm going to place handcuffs on you, and then we'll talk."

The boys and Clair had left their vehicle and were standing in a line behind the edge of the shed. Mr. Wagner stayed behind the wheel. Mike stepped out of the patrol car and backed Officer Satrang. It was too much for Bern. He dropped to his knees. "Es tut mir leid," he said in German. "Es tut mir leid!"

"Stand up!" Officer Satrang ordered.

He stood and was placed in handcuffs. Bern hung his head. "Es tut mir leid," he said again.

"You may be sorry, but only sorry you got caught! Let's go in," Officer Satrang said. "Let's have a look-see in this shed." On the way into the shed, the officer reminded Mike that hard work is not always good work. The rest followed, and Mr. and Mrs. Wagner watched through the door. The room was small, crowded, and stinky and crammed with pots, pans, tubs, and tables. "Okay, Bern, let's have it. We all know you did this; the evidence is right here. I think the judge in Bottineau County would be impressed with a confession. Why would you go through with all of this?" Officer Satrang asked.

Bern looked up and around at everyone in the room. He sneered at Mike and Levi, who were standing in the corner. Officer Satrang nudged him to begin talking

"I uze zee *Farmer's Almanac*. It told me good years of planting are coming. I need more land to farm zo I can make money. I have nephews who vant to farm, too. I vanted Gunder's land, but he vould not sell it to me. He is not uzing it. I zought he vould leave if he saw zee blue hares. He has told me zat story for years. I vas only playing a joke on him. I planned on paying him if he sold it."

"That is not a joke, Bern! You knew you were scaring him off of his own property!" Officer Satrang said. You really should be ashamed of yourself. You are under arrest for harassment, animal theft, and cruelty to animals."

"You zound like my vife, plus, Gunder has already told me I could buy it."

"No, I'm sorry, there will be no land sales. He told you that under duress. Plus, you've told people all over town that he's crazy. I don't think a court of law will uphold that type of dealing. You can't have it both ways, Bern. Let's go have a seat in the patrol car."

"Wait!" Mike suddenly yelled. "There are other questions. Where's Omi's other white rabbit? And I want to know if he dipped those rabbits in hot water. And where did he get the other rabbits?"

"I trapped zome hares on zee prairie, und I brushed zee dye on zee hares. One hare got avay from me. I let go of other blue hares in Gunder's glade. No more gueszions," Bern explained.

They quietly walked out of the building to the patrol car, and Officer Satrang took him away for the night. As the patrol car left and was out of sight, a thunderous applause erupted from the small crowd standing in the dark, near a small granary, in the middle of a North Dakota snow-covered field. Mike blushed, but the darkness camouflaged much of it. The boys pushed him around in a congratulatory way, and the adults were patting him on the back. He wished Omi could have seen it all.

The little building grew cold. They had let the heat out of the building, and Clair had cut the heating oil off which ran to the burners. Mrs. Wagner asked her husband to take them by Omi's house to see if her mother would let her come for a supper celebration at the diner. She only promised leftovers from the day's cooking, but everybody was hungry for a late snack and a warm place to be. The ride back to the diner would be full of stories from the week. Suddenly, Mike threw open the back car door. "Hold on," he said. "I'll be right back." He ran into the old shed, pulling off his right mitten. He came out as fast as he went in but was dripping blue dye in the snow.

"Why'd you do that to your mitten, Mike?" Mr. Wagner asked.

"I had to make a set," Mike replied as he held up his left one. The others laughed hard, and Levi threatened him if he touched his new coat with blue dye.

Arriving at Omi's home, Mrs. Wagner went to the front door. She explained the events of the night to her mother. She was excited to hear of the justice for Bern and wanted Omi to go and celebrate as well, but there was no room in the car. "One more won't hurt; come join us." Mrs. Wagner talked her into driving to the diner with Omi.

The following day, Mike and Omi rode with Officer Satrang to Gunder's farm to explain the events of the night before. "He called me this morning, kids. He's still talkin' about those blue rabbits. I can't wait to put this to rest," he said as he knocked on the door. Gunder answered the door and seemed anxious to speak but respectfully waited for the officer to finish. He appeared embarrassed about the matter and tried to suggest he knew what was going on.

"Ya ya, I tought so," he said. He disappeared into another room then reappeared holding a BB gun. It was the model 25, pump action BB gun Mike hoped he would earn. "You dit your part, Mike. I vant you to have dis even dough da hares are not really blue. I tink the bad times vill end for me now." The gun looked nearly brand new, and Gunder said that only a few shots had been fired from it. Mike took the gun from him slowly and reverently and turned it every which way.

"Thank you, Gunder!" he said in a happy tone. "I just can't believe it. I won't be shooting rabbits, though." Omi smiled at him.

Officer Satrang began again explaining why Bern had gone through so much trouble. He also

warned Gunder not to share with others his vulner-
abilities. "Let's keep the storytelling to a minimum,
Gunder. I think you got the whole town talkin'.
Some people take advantage of others when they
learn their weaknesses. It's a hard lesson to learn
sometimes," he said.

Omi placed her hand on Mike's back. "I am
proud of you. You did a good thing for Gunder
and me. I am naming my next two rabbits Gunder
and Mike."

"Oh, my!" Gunder replied as he laughed. Officer
Satrang laughed, too, and figuring he had worn
out his welcome, grabbed his coat and began saying his goodbyes. Gunder turned suddenly and
grabbed his coat as well. "Come see," he said as
he darted out the door ahead of Officer Satrang.
"Come, Mike, Omi."

Again, Gunder was running faster than an old
man should run, but the others were on his heels.
He led them into the barn and opened the tack
room's door. Sitting in a small trap was the bluest
rabbit Omi had ever seen. She had seen only two,
but it was definitely bluer than the last one.

"My little Waabooz! Oh, you got painted blue, too!" she cried. "How did you get it, Gunder?"

"I set da traps, too," he said. "I fount it dis morning in da trap."

"Oh, Gunder, thank you! I have all of my missing rabbits." She opened the cage door and cuddled it as before, staining her coat with more blue coloring. Officer Satrang shook his head with a large grin, and Mike smiled at Gunder as they left the barn.

The blue rabbit in Omi's arms matched the sky's color perfectly. It was a true cerulean blue. Gunder stopped for a moment. "My motter cried vhen she saw dat color. She missed her sveet Vigdis, and so do I."

Mike and Omi felt sad to hear Gunder speak about the loss of his little sister, but Officer Satrang quickly changed the subject and made a suggestion that sparked all of their attention. "You haven't done a lot with these trees in the past years. Why don't you get a sign in the yard and sell some. It's Christmas, for goodness sake!"

"We'll help, Gunder!" Mike said with excitement. There's still two weeks before Christmas, and we can sell a lot of trees. People around here would be happy to buy a tree from you. We still don't have a tree, and it would save us a trip. Nobody sells trees around here."

"I vould need help, of course," he answered.

"You have my word, Gunder." Mike stuck his hand out to shake. Gunder's rough hand grasped Mike's, and he shook it strongly with a large smile. Officer Satrang winked at Omi.

Mike and Omi wasted no time in making signs, and the other boys agreed to help. They secured old metal signs from Clair's storage room and repainted them with paint found in the old filling station under the nest. Mike's uncle, Clair, and Mr. and Mrs. Wagner pitched in, too. Within days a beautiful sign graced the front of Gunder's property along the East and West. Other signs were posted along the highways coming into town. News spread quickly through Willow City since the Iceberg Diner posted a large sign on the door offering free hot cocoa that came with handmade fliers courtesy of Omi. Clair handed out the fliers at the Cenex station, and Officer Satrang put out a dispatch to the other communities in the area.

Folks from all around seemed to remember Gunder's Christmas tree farm from years past and were eager to visit it again. It wasn't long before many read the new honorary sign in front of Gunder's home and purchased a tree. Only one thing had changed; a name had been added, reminding them all of someone special from Gunder's past.

Todd Gunderson

Todd R. Gunderson is a native of North Dakota. The stories he writes encompass experiences from his youth and places where he spent his time. Todd has twenty-four years of teaching experience in grades three–seven, and is currently teaching in an elementary school in Tennessee. He enjoys teaching the writing curriculum and interacting with his students. He loves seeing his students expand their writing abilities.

Todd is also a custom woodworker, and loves working with his hands. He is married with four children, and they all love the country life. He wishes to write books that a young person will not want to put down.

Follow the Willow City boys in:

The Hairy Farmer's Daughter
   Bronze IPPY award for Juvenile Fiction

A Limb Along the Railroad Tracks

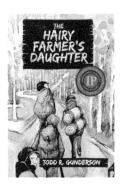 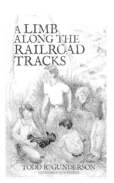

Inspirational fiction:

From Tangled Roots
   When Carrie's confusion over life decisions clouds her thinking, Uncle Wit tells her stories about her ancestors. It is through his inspiration and her kindness and integrity that a sweet elderly man named Edd, leaves her something that will change and fulfill her destiny.

Made in the USA
Monee, IL
12 November 2021

81924820R00111